THEN CAME MICHAEL

THEN CAME MICHAEL

CITY OF ANGELS SERIES

Sailor Penniman

DARROW PUBLISHING – LOS ANGELES | *AEQUALITAS*

Then Came Michael

Published in the United States by Darrow Publishing.

ISBN: 978-0-9993487-2-7

1 2 3 4 5 6 7 8 9 10

For those who are trying to figure it out

Other books by Sailor Penniman

Carry the One
The Ugly Post

∞ Chapters ∞

∞ Chapter 1 ∞

JAILHOUSE CLUES

"THIS IS BULLSHIT, AND YOU know it," the man said.

"I'm not gonna tell you again. Shut. Up. You have the right to remain silent. Use it."

Galen had thrown the man into the holding cell on a charge of aggravated vagrancy, although, technically, only the vagrancy part was a crime, and it was Galen who was aggravated, by the man.

He had spotted him in Grand Park in the middle of downtown L.A. The man appeared to harangue strangers with conversation. Galen asked him why he did that. The sight of his police uniform got the man's hackles up and his mouth moving. He delivered a mini-tirade about police oppression. He added a little verbal indecency—profane words Galen had forgotten existed—and leaned in a tad too much. Something about the way he entered Galen's space made Galen uneasy, and the man had ended up in cuffs. The way Galen saw it, the man had forced himself to be arrested.

No one had booked him. Booking involved too much paperwork. Galen just wanted the man to cool off before they let him back onto the street. Galen's best friend on the force, and in life, Chet, would start his shift as Galen clocked out. They would agree on a time to release the man, and that would be the end of it. No fingerprints, no record, no paperwork, no problems.

Galen checked his watch. He had two minutes left on his shift. He had hoped to set the man free in those same two minutes, to save Chet the hassle, but the man paced the cell and muttered more profanity.

"I want a lawyer," he said.

"So you can stick it to The Man, right?"

"I want a lawyer because it's my right, cop."

"You don't need one."

"Bullshit! If I'm in here, I need a lawyer!"

"I think you have that wrong."

Galen checked his watch again. Ninety more seconds. He headed for the door that led from the holding area to the public part of the station. He didn't get far.

"Don't walk away from me, cop."

Galen groaned, outwardly. He wanted the man to know he was irritating. He reached for the door. Seventy-five seconds from that moment, he would claim his checked weapon outside at the desk, change into civvies at his locker, get into his car, and aim it toward home, where he was sure his wife and gourmet takeout waited for him.

"What are you afraid of, cop?"

That did it. He turned and walked to the small holding cell.

The man stood six inches from the bars. Galen stood closer to the bars on his side. He had a rant ready. It would fill the final thirty seconds of his shift.

It didn't go as planned.

The man stepped closer to Galen and looked him in the eye. For a moment, for a flash, the man gave Galen pause, and in the strangest, most non-policeman-to-perp way.

Galen looked more closely at the man's eyes and at the rest of his face. His tan skin and dusty brown hair distracted Galen. His eyebrows were surprisingly neatly trimmed for someone who had let himself get arrested. The cleft in his chin that gave his face a symmetry made him seem organized and above it all.

Why did I arrest you, again?

Galen took hold of the bars, something he never did. Even with a vest on and the jailed guest thoroughly searched, Galen had seen over his years on the force hands suddenly around a cop's throat or spittle—or something worse—dripping from an officer's face. If his boss had seen him standing so close to the man, he'd have thrown Galen in his own cell for gross incompetence. Still, Galen held onto the bars a few inches from the man.

The man gripped the bars from his side and rested his hands just above Galen's. Galen didn't flinch or back away.

The two men almost touched. Galen felt the heat that bounced back and forth between their skin in the microscopic space that separated their hands.

The man didn't move or speak.

Galen leaned in half an inch. "Listen, uh, what was your name again?"

"Pshh." The man shook his head in genuine disappointment.

They were the same height—six feet in shoes—and Galen sensed right around his mouth the warm air the "pshh" had released from the man's mouth. Galen still didn't back away, not even as a reflex.

"You don't even know who you rounded up. This is such bullshit." The man snort-laughed. Galen felt more warm air. "Just call me Michael. Maybe I'll get out of here without you people putting too much of me in your cop tracker harassment system thing." The warm air smelled sweet.

"Whatever…," Galen said.

"Michael. Say it slowly. Mi-chael."

Galen came to. "Michael. Got it, smart man. When the other officer gets here—"

The door to the holding area opened.

"Dude. You still here?" It was Chet.

Galen looked at Michael for a few more seconds.

"No," he said to Chet while staring at Michael. "I'm outta here. He's yours."

He let go of the bars, and the tops of his hands brushed the soft bottoms of Michael's. The warm smoothness felt good to Galen. The sensation, in actual duration, lasted less than a second, but it hovered and lingered, like a strange, pleasant memory.

Galen turned and headed for the door.

"Wait," Michael said. "What about when the other officer gets here? Is this him? What do you mean?"

"You'll find out," Galen said over his shoulder. He left the holding area.

Michael shouted, "This is such bullshit!" Galen kept walking.

Galen heard Chet slam the door to the holding area and run to catch up to him. He had skipped picking up his gun and stormed on, to the locker room. He yanked off his uniform.

"Whoa, slow down," Chet said.

"Georgie's waiting. With a lot of good food. And I forgot my damned gun at the desk." He was rough on his locker. He threw things in it, snatched things out of it, and slammed it shut.

"Food? This late?"

"Life of a cop's wife. Hell, life of a nurse. We eat when the city and hospital say it's okay to eat. Brianna'll find out about the cop side of things soon enough, when you get up the courage to ask her." He had meant it as good-humored chatter, but it came out cranky.

Chet went along, anyway. "Hang on, there. Not too soon, if you please. Happy, unmarried coward, here. What do you want me to do with our guest?"

"Cut him loose when he can prove he's able to behave."

"It looked like he already proved it. You were standing right in his grill, trying to get fired. He didn't pull anything."

"Well, then cut him loose."

"Leaving me to hear all about what bullshit it is on his way out the door." Chet smiled.

"Yeah. Sorry. His stuff's in the usual spot."

"All right."

" 'Night."

" 'Night. And eat some buffalo wings or chow mein or whatever it is for me."

Normally, Galen would have chuckled, but he was still irritable from his face-down with Michael.

Michael. Say it slowly.

What was it about him that made me so mad and made me want to hang around his cell all night?

Galen picked up his gun and headed for his car, which was parked at a meter across the street from the station. He had staged it there earlier in the day, so it would be waiting for him.

His phone buzzed in his pocket.

I'm almost to my car. It's right there, across the street.

He checked the caller ID.

Georgie. He caught himself groaning again, even though he couldn't wait to get home. "Hi," he answered. "I'm just leaving."

Let's hang up.

"Well, we have a problem, Gay."

She called him "Gay" as a shortened version of Galen. She didn't mean it the way people shortened Jeffrey to Jeff or Patrick to Pat. She simply stopped saying "Galen" halfway through, like people who called guys named Ernie "Ern."

"We have no parmesan. Can you swing by Vons on the way home?"

"Vons? It's not in a good spot coming from here. Are you sure?"

"I'm sure. Come, on. I would say do it for the one you love, but I think I'll have better luck asking you to do it for your stomach." She laughed.

He smiled, but it was more politeness than joy. "Absolutely, Baby Girl. Vons, parmesan, home. Soon." He hung up the phone.

"So, they pay you to chit-chat, and right in front of the station, no less." The voice snickered. "Must be nice, cop."

Michael. Why are you standing right over my shoulder, so close to my ear I can smell your sweet breath? Why aren't I going all cop on you for breathing right down my neck?

"I see Officer Byrne let you go."

"He did. It was all bullshit."

"You made that clear. I'm sure you made it clear to him, too."

"I did."

"Good. I'm glad."

Galen waited for traffic to pass so he could jaywalk to his car.

"And now you people have kept me just late enough that I've missed the DASH that will get me to the Number Two. I figure I'll be home sometime after midnight."

"Call somebody." He sounded callous, but he felt bad. Once a person missed a DASH for the night, it could leave them stranded. The Metro buses ran late, but if a person was far from a route, a fifty-cent DASH ride would get them to their real bus stop. DASH buses shut down in the early evening. Without a DASH, a person may have to walk ghastly distances to find their bus.

"Can't 'call somebody.' " His voice hinted at air quotes around "call somebody". "My phone died while you had it in its own little lock-up. Putting the owner in jail for three hours will do that. And, anyway, half my friends are homeless. They don't have nine-hundred-dollar phones, and they haven't strung landlines through the tent cities on Spring Street or Sixth or San Julian, in case you hadn't noticed, which you should have, cop, or don't you serve and protect the good citizens in those tents?"

"Never mind. Forget I said anything." The road was clear, but Galen stayed on the police station side of the street. He stared at Michael. There was something familiar in the other man's face. He reminded Galen of himself, in coloring and height and build, but

Michael, *say it slowly, Galen,* had more, to Galen's eye, a handsomer face and a measured demeanor that aroused Galen's curiosity about what lay beneath it.

"No, I won't forget it," Michael said. "Why should I make it easy for you? This is your fault. If you had bothered to ask me why I was so-called loitering in Grand Park, you'd know that I was doing what I do lots of nights. I was gathering shopping lists, the dire stuff, for people who are homeless, the things that make the difference between bleeding all night from a stupid cut or putting a Band-Aid on it. I was gonna run that stuff down and distribute it before it got too late and everybody zipped themselves in for the night. I do it several times a week, which you might know if you cared about the people on your beat. You might have seen me." He shook his head.

More disappointment.

"Because of you," he continued, not yet spun out, "I have no idea what people need or even which tents some of them are in, and you've dragged me *way* off the path of the Number Two."

"I'm sorry, but there's nothing we can do about that. What about the other half of your friends? The ones who aren't homeless?" He offered his phone. "Here. You're welcome to call anybody from this."

Michael contemplated the phone. For the first time in more than three hours, he looked less annoyed, but not by much.

"No, thanks. They're in halfway houses or at work or asleep. *It's late.* And there's no way I'm putting their numbers into a cop's phone."

Galen frowned. His feelings were hurt, but he tried not to show it.

"I'll figure it out," Michael said. His tone had softened a measure. He had a problem and, it seemed, no time to press his gripes with the police. "Thanks, anyway." He started down the street.

Galen called after him. "You're really gonna play the guilt card, aren't you?"

"Yep," he said. He never turned around.

Damn.

Galen waited for cars to pass in the road and jogged across the street to his car. He stashed his gun in a lockbox in his trunk, hopped in the car, and started the motor. He waited for more cars to pass, made a U-turn, and drove until he pulled alongside Michael.

Michael walked on.

Galen rolled down the window on the passenger side. "Where do you live?" He inched the car along at two miles an hour.

"I told you, I take the Two." Michael said. He never slowed down.

"The Two covers a lot of ground."

"Well, the ground I'm interested in is WeHo."

"West Hollywood."

"West Hollywood. Say it slowly. West. Hol-ly-*wood*."

A full minute passed. Michael walked, and Galen inched.

"This is dumb. Get in."

Michael stopped.

Galen stopped.

"Get in."

"Don't you have anywhere to be?"

Georgie. Vons. Parmesan. For the one he loved.

"Not really. Get in."

"All right, cop." Michael opened the door and the overhead light came on inside the car. Michael's neat eyebrows and tan skin and cleft chin were in full view. Galen watched him as he shut the door and buckled his seatbelt.

"And quit calling me that. It's Galen. Say it slowly. Ga-len."

They looked right into each other's eyes as the light faded. A moment after the light went out, they burst out laughing.

∞ Chapter 2 ∞

SEVENTEEN

GALEN WOULD BE IN TROUBLE with Georgie. He heard it in her voice when he called her from West Hollywood to say he had been sidetracked by work and would lose even more time if he stopped at Vons for parmesan cheese.

She had said she had figured as much and that he could forget the cheese since the food would be two hours old by the time he made it home, and she would be in bed, with a full stomach and no parmesan cheese.

He didn't understand himself. She was easygoing. Few things upset her. They had been married five years, and he knew what those things were. He had no idea why he walked into conflict with her when he had complete control over arriving on time and keeping her happy.

He couldn't use Michael as an excuse, even if he was the reason Galen wasn't at home eating a spread of Italian food.

"You don't have to take me home," Michael had said. "Any of these bus stops along Sunset will get me there. Just drop me at the next one, and I'm good."

That had been Galen's chance. He had even had the same thought several blocks earlier and watched himself pass bus stops without dropping off Michael, refusing to take the out, because something he didn't understand compelled him to keep driving.

"It's all right. You lost three hours with me. Can't have you waiting for a bus and then, when you finally get on one, stopping every couple of blocks. Plus, you'll have to walk that last stretch when you get off, and you'll lose more time."

But that wasn't it. He heard himself deliver that excuse but didn't believe it. He reflected for half a mile and came up with something that made no sense: He liked being near Michael. He had even liked it in the jail, where Michael had insulted him on professional and personal levels. The drive home gave him the chance to remain in Michael's orbit, and he took it.

"Go figure. You cops. I swear."

The words were snarky but not the tone. Since Michael had gotten into Galen's car and they had made it through those awkward first moments of inane small talk and tapping Michael's address into the GPS and working their way from downtown over to Sunset Boulevard, where Michael could catch the Number Two, he had lost his rancor.

"Well, now's your chance," Galen said, when they were still far less than halfway to Michael's house, according to Galen's GPS.

"Uh, you have to be clearer than that."

"To explain why you were in the park. Buried in the 'bullshits' you dished at the police station, I picked up on you doing some good works. Am I right?"

"You *were* listening." He smiled.

"I was." Galen grinned and turned on the radio. "Well?"

"I run a nonprofit organization in West Hollywood that fights homelessness and tries to ease the way for homeless people. It's more complicated, but that's basically it."

"Aren't there more homeless people downtown than in WeHo?"

"Here comes the complicated part. Technically, yes, but it's better if we're away from downtown. Otherwise, we'd get every person with a minor gripe asking us to solve it. There are a lot of layers to what we do, and we're actually more effective from a distance."

"Really? That's strange for me since I'm only effective up close and personal."

"For us, it depends on where we are in the timeline of someone's problems. The only way to have some control over how we help people and dedicate our resources is to send staff and volunteers out to the various homeless camps and all over the streets and run recon and ask people what they need. We come back to home base and work it out. It's a bit unconventional until they get to know us—they always think we're going to bail on them or maybe come back and rob them until they see it play out and we know them better, and then they're usually okay, for the most part. Some people just don't trust us. We work through it."

"That's pretty innovative, to find the people in need instead of hoping they somehow find you."

Michael smiled. "Thanks. I think so. And not to sound like a fund-raising pitch, but we provide every kind of supply you can think of, and we help displaced people find family around the country, get folks enrolled in literacy and GED programs, that kind of thing. We assist veterans and others with job searches. We may stop what we're doing and get someone literally off the sidewalk and into hospice care. And, we fight with people who fight addiction if it will help them."

"I have those same fights," Galen said, "when it escalates to criminal activity or people put themselves in danger. Drugs, sex, bad relationships, shoplifting, you name the addiction. I think I've arrested the full array of people dealing with habits, and it's always so hard when their codependents beg me not to take them. Do you get that, too?"

"All the time."

The GPS said, "Continue straight onto Hollywood Boulevard," at the point where Sunset Boulevard split and remained

Sunset Boulevard if Galen veered left and turned into Hollywood Boulevard if he went straight.

"That's correct," Michael said. "You're good."

They were both quiet as Galen went through the light and stayed on Hollywood Boulevard.

The mini-ceremony of making sure they were going the right way over, Michael said, "I think the hardest for us is when we're dealing with domestic violence and we have to swoop in and help someone find a shelter. If they have kids, it becomes mission-critical, but we can't help one parent kidnap the kids from the other parent, so it gets sticky. Sometimes, we walk away and leave someone where they are. Those are my hardest days."

"That's weird. Those are my worst calls, too, by far. I get them pretty much every night. Thank goodness we're not in the days when the victim could say, 'It's okay. I'm not in danger,' and the police had to leave, knowing the person was totally at risk and might even face the worst of it, ever, as soon as we left. Now, if we have probable cause of a crime committed, it's over."

"That's when I don't mind cop— *policemen*," Michael said.

Galen smiled. "Glad to know we make the cut, sometimes."

"*Sometimes.* I mean, we keep an extra close eye on gay homeless folks. It can really be homophobia unleashed out there. People are always happy to tear up people who have no doors they can lock. Gay, lesbian, trans, they're all vulnerable to people going off, and, a few times, the police were our friends. Broke stuff up and put enough fear into people to lay off us. I say, 'Us,' because I'm gay, too."

"I'm sorry to say I've seen that side of the streets. It's disgusting. I'm glad we were there. And, fund-raising pitch aside," he smiled, "it sounds like the place where you work would fold up without you."

"I don't know. I technically manage everything—it's my foundation, although my name's not on it—so in some ways, I guess you're right. We each wear several hats, though. Nonprofit, and all. I probably wear more hats than anyone else." He laughed pleasantly.

Galen felt guilty for foiling Michael's efforts that night. Inexplicably, he was also glad to hear Michael was gay.

He had stared at Michael through the dark car as he shared that information. The familiarity coming from the other face returned. Features he usually saw in the mirror stared back at him, although Galen thought Michael had looks to which Galen could only aspire.

Michael's cleft chin was the most obvious differentiator, but Michael also smiled with more mischief, and his eyebrows seemed to guard a very bright mind that filled his eyes with whimsy and a little daring.

Galen hadn't thought much about his own eyes, but he thought they were more like ones that asked questions and revealed his curious nature. He was a cop because he was curious, and not the other way around. And his smile held no mysterious layers, which gave him a frankness and made him approachable, he had been told by his superior officers, who sometimes put his friendly demeanor to use to make headway with suspects before they landed in interview rooms. Those differences aside, Michael's countenance reminded Galen of his own.

Maybe that's why I'm still driving along Hollywood Boulevard, why I want to be here with Michael instead of at home with Georgie. Maybe this is a strange, short journey of self-exploration.

"So, is that what you want to be when you grow up? An...avenger—I'm serious—for folks who are struggling? Or is this a stop on the way to a job with one of those huge charities we see on TV?"

"Well, I'm thirty-two—"

"Which I didn't know because I never booked you—no record," he said. He flashed a modest smile.

"Which is only an issue because—"

"I know. The bullshit."

Michael grinned. "Okay, I'll drop it. Where was I?"

"Your TV job."

"Which I'll actually never have. I've been at this for ten years, since I finished college. I'm in, at the local level, until they wipe out homelessness on these mean streets." He glanced out the window at Hollywood Boulevard. "And since I'm in charge where I am now—I built it, and it's mine, really—I see no reason to leave. I get to shape policy and do things my way. I don't have to convince some stubborn penny-pincher where the struggle is. I just gotta convince me. And I came to the party convinced, so that part's easy."

"I admire your convictions. I don't know that I'm as noble, but I get the dedication. I'm thirty-three, been a cop—I can say it, you can't—" he said, and he grinned, "since I was twenty-two, too."

He hesitated. He wondered if he should say what had popped into his head. Usually, his brain shut down his mouth if it started to bring up the subject that always lurked just around corners in his mind, hoping for a chance to step out and take the stage, but driving along with Michael in the quiet confines of the car, he felt reassured, somehow, and less restrained by his usual need to protect himself.

He took a chance. "My parents were killed in a home invasion when I was seventeen," he said, "and I've wanted to be on this side of crime ever since. No question."

That wasn't so bad.

"My goodness. I'm so sorry."

"Thanks." Galen looked out of the window in front of him, but he saw much farther than what was before him. He saw all the way into his past and became a little wistful. He wondered why he had brought up his parents.

"Did it happen here? In L.A., I mean?"

"Yeah, but I try to keep it separate in my mind. It's been a long time. I miss them, but I don't think about it every day, like I used to. The first two years were the worst. A long nightmare." He laughed a little awkwardly. "Sorry. I don't know why I brought this up."

"No, don't apologize. You asked me what I do in my job. In a way, it's this. I hear people's histories. Please don't apologize."

"Thanks. And, you know, thankfully, I'm in a different place. I guess I found ways to cope. And therapy, which I fought like a typical teenager," he said, and he couldn't believe he had revealed that fact. He wasn't ashamed, but he usually kept that door shut because of all of what lay behind it.

"I can imagine," Michael said. "I can imagine." He subtly reached up and turned the radio down a little.

The door's open, now, Galen.

"Now? I'm grateful for it every day."

They were both quiet, and Galen could tell without looking that Michael's silence was comfortable without expectations. He listened without judgment or anticipation of details.

Galen watched three cars pass his car and change lanes to move in front of him, but he couldn't react and speed up. Something about Michael's demeanor and presence slowed everything down for Galen.

"In that struggle with therapy, what do you think turned it around?" Michael asked, which was a thoughtful question Galen never heard from people who found out about his parents. "You said it helped but that you fought it, too. Do you mind if I ask what the turning point was?"

Galen knew the answer without having to consider the question too long. He had asked himself the same question years earlier.

"I learned to cope with what happened," he said, "and I guess I gave therapy the credit, and it kept me going back. I learned to deal with the violence of it and the violation, the lack of any control over it, the anger, the massive void. All those times you go to tell your parents something or ask them something or wonder what they think about something, and they're not there. Every, single time. And then you remember why, and you feel for them and you want to hurt people. Fortunately, I got past that after a couple of years. But it took consistent therapy to get me there, and I guess somewhere in there, I saw that. Eventually, I got more than just the healing. It ingrained in me that I wanted to be a cop. Or maybe joining law enforcement was a kind of therapy."

Michael was quiet.

"Don't get me wrong. It wasn't that linear."

"I didn't think it was. Lots of back and forth and success and sudden regression and jumping around on the map, I'm sure."

How did you know?

"Yeah, and not understanding what had magnitude and getting blindsided by something you thought you had figured out."

Michael turned the music all the way down.

"I missed my dad, you know, right after, just being able to talk in shorthand, but, over time, I really missed my mom something fierce," he heard himself say. He sounded louder to himself without the radio playing.

Or maybe it's the words.

"She was the only person who really got my jokes." He smiled a little. "That's sort of the one thing I never got back. I know how to laugh, but I don't have much of my own sense of humor anymore."

"I'm really sorry, Galen."

"No, no worries." He smiled. "I really only brought it up to say that I know what it means to be passionate about what you do. I used to dream about catching the guys and putting the cuffs on them. And that was after...."

Michael waited and then probed, gently. "After...."

"After toning it down a notch from thinking about catching them at something and taking them out in a shootout." He glanced at Michael.

A moment passed. "I understand," Michael said. "Not just saying that. I get it. I like to help people with all the support in the world, but the other side of the coin of all the unfairness, sometimes, is raw outrage. I've had to rein myself in more than once."

Galen smiled. "Eventually, I was okay with just being a police officer. I grew up, you know?"

"Were they ever caught?"

"Yeah, but not tied up in a neat bow. There were two guys. Each went on to have different criminal careers. They caught one when he was arrested for domestic violence, and they took his D.N.A. It...matched. Later, the second one was shot at the scene of a store robbery after he brandished a weapon."

"Did—"

"No, not me."

"And it was him? The second one, I mean? For sure?"

"Yeah. The fingerprints and D.N.A. matched. It was him. They got 'em both."

Michael nodded and rode along silently, contemplating, Galen figured, the seeming justice of both perpetrators being caught.

He shifted a little in his seat. "Do you mind if I ask...?"

"How I survived?"

Galen had answered that question dozens of times in the early years, when he had less control over the subject of his parents' murders coming up in conversation. It was the first thing people asked.

"I was away on a school trip when it happened. Instead of my mom waiting in the parking lot to meet the bus when we got back, the principal picked me up."

Michael took in an audible breath, a long, quiet, almost-gasp, in a spontaneous display of sympathy and understanding of the significance of what Galen had just said. The only thing missing was the, "Oh, my god," that it implied. He sat so still, he seemed to hold that one breath as he listened to Galen's story.

"I thought I was in trouble. I wish I would have been, that it had been just that. That was the haziest time. I moved around in a daze. Our house was a crime scene. I stayed with my grandparents, but I wanted to go back there. I didn't really believe it and wanted to see it for myself, you know?"

Michael nodded. "I do."

Galen traveled ten or fifteen miles under the speed limit and kept talking.

"And, I had no clothes. Just the stuff I had on the trip, but, for me, those things were tainted. They were what I was wearing while I was gone, and it was all happening, and what I had on when I found out. I couldn't take the sight of them. I wanted to go home and get different clothes. My grandfather finally took me shopping. It was the saddest thing, ever. While we were there, he bought me a suit. For the funerals."

"Oh, god. That's…awful."

"It was."

"And, I'm sorry for the dumb question, but you said, 'Funerals.' You had to go through that twice? I mean, you weren't able to have one service?"

"Not a dumb question, at all. No, we couldn't. My mom's autopsy. The coroner. He didn't…release her for over a month. It was twelve days for my dad. We laid him to rest, and then a lot of the same family came back for my mom's service. It was the year I grew a lot, though, so my suit didn't fit anymore."

"Oh, no...."

"Yeah. My grandfather and I went back to the store."

"Wow...."

"But I was able to finally go back to the house in that in-between time."

"Was it...cleaned up by then?"

"That's the weird thing. You have to clean it yourself. The police don't do that. They take what they need as evidence—no matter how valuable or personal—and leave the rest, including the fingerprint dust."

"Damn."

"Yeah. My grandfather came to the rescue, again. He hired some people to do industrial cleaning before I went back. He had to let them in and oversee it all, the straightening of the furniture, the clean-up of blood stains and broken glass, everything. It took two days. I don't know how he didn't die by the end of it."

"I'm speechless. I just can't even imagine."

"It's okay. It is hard to imagine, even for me. Sometimes, I still can't believe it happened, even while my brain has accepted it."

"What happened to the house? I mean, since you were still a minor, and all."

"Long story short, I inherited it. My parents had a will, which was weird for them, but in hindsight, I guess not. They were responsible people. My grandparents—they're my mom's parents—kept it up through probate, and then they helped me sell it. That was complicated. Lawyers and whatnot. I folded the money into a trust I never touched. Would have felt weird using that money. And my grandparents arranged that specifically so that I'd have a safety net, so it was better that way, the not touching it, I mean. It's still sitting there, growing. I might give it to my kids, if I ever have any."

Georgie's been talking about kids. Some days, it sounds great. Other days, I don't know.

He shook those thoughts. "I used the insurance money to pay for college and living expenses. I figured that was different. That was the point of the insurance, and I thought my parents would want me to use that money for school since they weren't there to, you know, put me through college."

He changed lanes for no reason.

"So, you stayed in L.A.? Your grandparents must have liked having you there with them."

You're the first person who didn't add, "To remind them of their daughter." You can't replace people who die.

"They did, but they were too old for the day-to-day. They couldn't quite pull it off. I mean, I wasn't your typical seventeen-year-old by then. I was a hot holy mess. And they were, too. I left L.A. and finished my senior year in Denver, with an aunt and uncle."

"Was that hard? Leaving your friends during what you were going through?"

"You know, other than a therapist, no one's ever asked me that." He glanced at Michael and smiled, just a little, almost sadly, to express appreciation. "It was hard. I missed my friends and my grandparents. I worried about my grandfather a lot. People moved me around and took care of me, but I think they thought as long as I was living and breathing and there to begin with, the details were less important."

"I guess that's human nature, but that's hard."

"It was very hard, but my Aunt Jeanine actually saved me that day she insisted I move in with them. When I got to Denver, she was the one who pushed for constant therapy and took me to those appointments whether I liked it or not." He smiled a little again. "She's technically an aunt by marriage—she's married to my dad's brother—but she fought for me like blood. And they came out here

with me when I started college, and my aunt dug in and made sure I
signed up with a doctor and found a therapist. And they didn't fight
my coming back here. Maybe in their way, they recognized my
friends were here. I think they thought dorm life in my own town
would help, even though my closest buddy, Noah, went to college in
Boston."

"Noah?"

"Yeah. He's a lawyer back east. I was bummed he was gone,
but coming back helped. I felt like I was doing what my parents and I
had talked about, although I changed my major from poli sci to
A.J.—administration of justice—and joined the force right after
graduation. The law, good or bad, is all I've ever known."

It had a been a long time since Galen had mentioned or even
thought about Noah, the person for whom he left the security of the
only family he had, who, in the end, wasn't there. Their status as best
friends hadn't survived the murders, the ball of despair that Galen
was, or the distance.

"Did that first guy go on trial?"

"He did. Made me sick. I was a sophomore in college by then."

"Did you have to testify?"

The GPS sent Galen into the beginnings of the nooks and
crannies of WeHo.

"I did, but just for a few questions, to establish that I wasn't
home, that my parents had no enemies, that we had no alarm
system, that kind of thing."

"Goodness."

"The penalty phase was…better, if you can call it that. I got to
finally tell a judge what those bastards had cost so many people. My
grandmother barely survived being the one to discover my parents,
the day after. I got to tell a judge that and more. I got to look the guy
in the face and tell him what I thought. My therapist helped me
prepare my statement."

Michael said, "I told you, I can get outraged. I don't know how you didn't choke him to death, and I'm not even for the death penalty, but that's brutal, having to be in the same room with him."

"It wasn't easy, but at least I have an honest life on my side. He has a life stretch at Pelican Bay."

"And a hard stretch," Michael said. "They don't mess around there, fancy name aside. I know from my halfway house travels."

"Yeah, it's definitely the roughest stint in California."

Michael glanced at the GPS. "Oh, it's better if you turn left at the street before the light," he said.

"Okay." Galen made the turn, and his GPS narrated itself restructuring the route. Galen wished it would be quiet.

Michael said, "You can cut that, if you want. I'll get us there." He rattled off some quick directions that Galen, as a cop, easily absorbed and retained. He usually only used the GPS as a backup on weird calls to places he'd never been. He had used it that night thinking it would make Michael's life easier. He was relieved to just get some real-life directions

Galen smiled. "Thanks."

"Don't take this the wrong way," Michael said, "but I would think you would be a detective by now."

"I have enough time on the books and have even passed the tests, mostly to prove to my superiors that I'm capable, so they'll leave me alone. But I declined the assignment. On purpose. I've racked up seniority in uniform, and I pretty much pick my patrols, and I go alone. And if a fracas starts, I have the freedom to be first on the scene, if I can get there."

Then he confessed a truth he rarely admitted. "And, honestly, it's not something I talk about much, but I'm not sure I wouldn't think about my parents if I were working detailed crimes that needed solving all day long, where you spend weeks and months on a case staring at the same crime scene photos. I'd see far more homicide. In uniform, it's more about prevention, keeping the peace, even rescue. Maybe secure a crime scene to be sure they get the evidence to catch the perps. I'm in an okay place about my mom and dad. Best to leave it alone."

He changed lanes and became quiet.

Michael was quiet, too.

"Probably sounds weak, but I'm okay with that. Therapy long ago set me free from caring about superficial things like other people judging me without knowing what they're talking about."

"It doesn't sound weak at all," Michael said. "It sounds sane and like therapy really worked. You seem to have a good sense of yourself and what your boundaries are."

Galen smiled with gratitude again and with a little pride. He had worked hard to know himself and admit what he could and couldn't handle. His aunt and uncle really had saved his life making sure he got help.

"Like I said," Michael said, "I meet so many people on the street who suffered trauma and found no way to cope. It's why they're there. It's tragic. Anybody can get hit and not find the help they need and just unravel and end up stranded. I see it every day."

"Me, too. You really gotta fight for your own sanity. For years, no one would tell me what really happened that night. I testified at the trial, but I wasn't in the courtroom for any of the rest of the trial. My aunt nixed it. I was an adult, but she put her foot down. She was right, but, later, I had to know. I had to see what I was trying to move past. You can't know where the land mines are if you don't enter the battlefield. I didn't want to bump into something down the road that turned out to be real trouble for my peace of mind that I didn't see coming."

Michael stared at Galen and waited.

"When I became a cop, I pulled the file. I was twenty-two."

Michael didn't say anything.

"It was bad, worse than I thought. My mom…. They killed my dad first. She was by herself with them, long enough for, you know…."

Michael remained quiet.

"I think not only about her but about my dad. He probably died trying to prevent that. It would…kill him to know he couldn't save her, that she had suffered. And I think about how much, on reflex, I wanted to talk to them about things after they were gone, even when I knew it was impossible. Your mind forgets, you know? In that moment, that must have happened to my mom. She lost my father and had to cope with that, and then she was very helpless, probably searching for him, out of habit, out of love, out of need, to talk about what was happening, to talk about what would happen to me, with them gone, and ask, in some weird sense of wanting to take care of business, how they could call my grandmother and tell her not to come by the next morning for church so that she wouldn't find them, and he wasn't there to talk it over with her. And, so, she was reminded again, just moments after it happened, that he had died, young, before his time, with a family he left behind, and of how he had been killed—with a garrote held fast by a doorknob—"

Michael drew in a short, hard gasp. "No…."

"Yeah. And she was reminded that she was alone. And she probably needed his strength, once he could no longer defend her and she was at their mercy, and his advice to look away, to avert her eyes, to pretend she was somewhere else during the worst of it, and she didn't have him."

Galen took a deep breath.

You've almost told the whole story. Just finish.

"And I'm sure she looked and saw his death and her own violation and impending death and couldn't escape anywhere far enough away in her mind while she suffered. I had stopped therapy by the time I pulled the file, but I needed another year of it to deal with how alone my mother was at the end, how confusing and cruel it all was, how much she had to process in a short time, while enduring torture and facing a certain death and not getting to say goodbye to me."

Michael listened without moving.

Finish, Galen. Tell him the rest. Say it all.

"It took me years to finally accept that it was a fraction of an overall good life. And that she would feel some relief knowing I had escaped, that I would be on that trip for twenty-four more hours and nowhere near the threat, even though I felt guilty about that, in the beginning. I figured if my dad and I had both been there, all three of us would have had a shot at surviving. I really struggled with that during the trial, when they went out of their way to prove means based on my absence. By the time I pulled the file, though, my training had taught me that once they surprise you and take down just one of you, it could be over anyway. They take advantage of people's panic and their initial frantic thoughts about protecting each other and sacrificing and the fact that they don't work in a like-minded way about how to get out of it. Lots of cases of whole families being held hostage. Eventually, I told myself what I thought my mom would have said to me, if she could, about not feeling guilty. I had the conversation for her. Still do, sometimes."

Michael nodded, seeming to agree with Galen's solution.

"And, I don't have any cliché, bad-B-movie memories to deal with, where the last words I spoke were something angry that I have replay every day with regrets. It was the opposite. I was going on that trip, and she had packed everything just so, and it all smelled like fresh laundry, and she stashed my favorite snacks that I wouldn't be able to get on the trip in a side pocket that I could tap into all weekend, which I did. She drove me to the bus and hugged me and said, 'I love you.' Because I was going away, while we hugged, she added a quick 'mom' kiss on the cheek. The very last words she spoke to me were, 'Have fun,' as the bus drove off. I heard her through the open window, and we were waving at each other."

After seeming to wait to be sure Galen had nothing to add, Michael said, "I'm relieved for you that you have that memory and not the bad-B-movie one."

And thanks for not saying, I'm "glad" you have that memory.

"Thank you. I appreciate that. And, you know, I've tried to live the life she would have hoped I could have if she had had to jump in the way and kill people to save me from that night, so I could live it. And, somehow, I slowly moved on. Except for her birthday. I can get through any of the other three hundred and sixty-four days in the year just fine. Holidays, my dad's birthday, Father's Day, even Mother's Day because I've made my peace there. But there's something about my mother's birthday, the day she was born, that's very had to get through when I think of her death. Even the days before and after, I'm pretty okay. But on the day, I get hit. Every, single year. I guess no therapy is perfect."

Michael watched him quietly, but Galen didn't feel scrutinized, as though he were a spectacle. He appreciated that Michael understood what most people hadn't in those first years, when he was younger, and strangers who met him and assumed his parents were alive—parents of his friends, teachers in Denver, schoolmates—naturally asked about them. When he explained, they tended to offer words like, "At least they're not suffering." But they had suffered brutally in the end, enough for a lifetime, even if it hadn't lasted long when measured over a lifespan. And, "They would be so proud of you," something he wished every hour he could prove for real. Or, "They loved you," words that meant well but that were often subconsciously designed to make the other person, and not Galen, feel better and get them through the hard conversation.

Galen appreciated people's kind words, but they usually accidentally hijacked his airing his feelings, and he ended up having to tend to their shocked feelings, instead. His therapists had taught him that it was okay to decline conversation that didn't help and that he owed no one the politeness of discussing the murders and the aftermath just because they had shown social politeness and inquired. Even genuine interest could be rebuffed, if necessary, they told him.

Not having to dread the topic because he was empowered to shut it down saved his sanity and allowed him to get through moments, first, and then life.

Michael seemed to know silence was the best way to show support. It meant the person really listened, for the sake of the person talking. He had taken Galen's side of the conversation at face value instead of as a horrible story to rush through with platitudes. Galen found it unique.

He was grateful. Their conversation was the most Galen had talked about his parents' murders since those early years of counseling. With Georgie, he stuck to occasional stories from childhood. He never talked about his parents' deaths or how the event made him feel. She had assumed he had arrived in a place where he no longer needed to talk about it.

"I can bet you're good with people on the street," Galen said. "You have a knack for listening. I'm sorry to drone on. It just came tumbling out." He laughed a little self-consciously.

"Not at all. I'm honored you shared. I can guess you only scratched the surface, let alone, did you drone on."

They glanced at each other and held their gazes for as long as Galen could safely keep his eyes off the road.

"Hearing you…it's a testament to what help and counseling can do. I wish the people I helped had found similar support long before I met them. They may not have needed me. I know it wasn't easy for you and that it's probably still not easy, and I think that's the point. You've put time into working through it because you know it's not easy. And you have some coping mechanisms to get through the harder days. Just knowing there will be hard days is so important. You have to be ready. That's how a person gets there. Sounds like you've struck a balance. You're in law enforcement, but you're not bombarded with reminders."

"Not too much. I see some wicked stuff, but not daily."

"Any siblings? Didn't sound like it, but just wondered."

"No, just me."

"That had to be even tougher."

It was. Thank you for not hiding from it. No one except my therapists have ever acknowledged that.

"It was. My mom and dad and I were a tight little family. I was finally not so obnoxious," he smiled a little, "and we were a team. I was on their committee."

"A lot of only children end up as part of management with their parents."

Galen smiled. "I like that. And it's true. I helped decide a lot of things. I guess that stuck. I'm independent. Had to be. But sometimes you wish you had more people around who had your back, who knew you coming and going and even needed you around because of who you were. With my parents, I wasn't incidental. My family took me in, but I knew I wouldn't have been there if my parents hadn't died."

He didn't say more. He had married into a large family, which had helped, but for some reason, he didn't want to mention that he was married. And he wasn't sure the voids he talked about had been filled by his marriage, but he left that unsaid, too.

He thought he should change the subject, so he did, to WeHo and politics and the harder aspects of working with people on the streets. They even found things to laugh about.

They drove with the windows down and talked so easily, Galen hadn't seen the blocks go by. He had slowly forgotten that Georgie had food waiting at home. He hadn't eaten, but he wasn't hungry. He felt filled and fulfilled.

He was sorry when they arrived at Michael's apartment, even if he was enamored with the look of it. It was a four-story Art Deco building with a 1930s charm.

"*Nice,*" Galen said.

"I guess I do all right." Michael smiled.

Galen said, "It has kind of an old-movie feel. It's quaint."

"Quaint? Did a policeman just say, 'Quaint,' to me?" Michael chuckled.

"We're full of surprises." Galen grinned wide.

"I see you are." Michael grinned too. "It's an old building but refurbed for real. Eight units. Quiet. *Quaint.*" His smile got bigger. "Two units on each floor, one unit on each side of the hallway down the middle."

"Wow." Galen craned to look at the building. "So, they run the length of the building, to the back, and almost half the width, going across? Damn."

"The hallway is kind of nineteen-thirties wide and eats into a little on each side, and there's an old spiral staircase at the end, and an elevator with a brass door. They take up a tad of space at the very back, but, yeah, the units are roomy, and the front doors are big. Word is, one of the big movie studios built it way back in the day, for contract players who lived with other actors as roommates. Every unit has five bedrooms, three large bathrooms, major closet space and nooks and crannies and other old-timey storage, and a huge kitchen. Art Deco tiles in all the common areas. I'm up on three, on that side." He pointed to the left of the building. "Bit of a view. Good neighbors. We're not creative, though, like our predecessors. Attorneys and accountants and…me, go figure," he said, and he smiled. "If you knew our front-door code, you'd laugh. But I guess I shouldn't tell even the police our code."

"You know us. We'll get in, one way or the other."

"Total bull—"

"Don't say it."

They laughed.

"You been here long?"

"Just two years. I got in at the right time, when it was still a bit rundown and they hadn't gentrified the area, yet. And I will never capitulate and call it a condo, even if that's what they called it when they sold it to me."

"Apartment? Say it slowly?"

They smiled.

"Yes," Michael said. "Apartment. Sounds more film noir."

They stared out the windshield for a moment, neither saying anything.

"In some ways, it was silly to move here, though."

"Why?"

"Well, it's pretty big for one person. I guess I had envisioned starting a family here," he smiled wistfully at the building, "but I forgot that families don't come with real estate. You have to work to build them." He smiled in a way that said he knew somewhere along the way he had missed something obvious that he finally understood, too late. It was a smile that said, "Oh, well."

"So…no husband or kids? As you say, didn't sound like it, but you never know."

Michael stared again at the building. "No. I worked so hard trying to make it to the destination, I didn't take the time to stop and meet that one traveler who might continue the journey with me. I arrived alone." He shrugged, as though willing to accept his fate, but his shoulders moved slowly and seemed to bear a great weight, as though he were burdened by the truth he spoke.

"I've thought about adopting," he said, "but I don't know. Not sure I want to do it alone, even if I *would* like to raise a little political warrior." He smiled a little deviously, but his expression said he was joking. "A child who's already here seems less gratuitous on my part. Someone brought it into the world. It's going to have a destiny. I might as well mold it—him or her—to be a good and fair citizen." He shrugged again, a little easier. "But, again, I don't know."

"Well, at least if it happens," Galen fanned out his hand as though he were displaying the apartment building as a game show prize, "you're ready." He smiled. "You planned well."

"I guess that's true."

"My turn to ask a 'don't take it the wrong way' question."

"Shoot," Michael said. "Well, not literally." He smiled.

Galen chuckled. "Whew. You caught me just in time. I was about to follow orders." He grinned. He surprised himself. He wasn't used to telling jokes. "Seriously, though, do you mind if I ask how you swung this? Seems expensive. Sorry if that's rude."

"Not at all. It's true. It was tough. I mean, my foundation does well. I pound hard for large donations. The artist community, Hollywood, some likeminded corporate folks, and private citizens really give us a lot of support. Ninety-three percent of it goes directly toward funding people and services, but we still make very decent salaries. I take the bus for environmental and social reasons and not financial ones. Some of my best research about how homeless people move about comes from simply riding the bus."

Galen nodded in appreciation.

"But people tend to spend what they make, and I guess I got smart early and refused to fall into that trap. I cinched my belt tight and basically bled trying to swing it, as you say. I lived in a tin can for *years* saving for the right place, waiting for it to come along. I don't usually tell people, but I ate a lot of ramen and pasta and corn flakes and some fruit and the cheapest produce I could find and P, B, and J, and not much else, for a lot of years. Took no vacations. Didn't join anything that cost money. Never had cable. Just a TV with an antenna and the newspaper. Came to the cell phone party *way* late. Survived on one wardrobe for about a decade. I'm not a miser, but I saved with a vengeance to get here as free and clear as possible. I was almost able to pay cash for it, and now I have those other things too. I'm finally using my paychecks for more than saving for this apartment. And I'm lucky. My mom— Oh, I'm sorry."

Galen grinned and felt a warmth he hoped showed. "Don't be. It's great that you have your mom. And, it's been years. I'm totally good with mom stories. In fact, I probably enjoy them more." He paused for emphasis then said, "What were you going to say?"

Michael stared at Galen for a moment before he finished. "Nothing really. Just that she gave me a little no-strings money cushion to give me some breathing room. A replenishment of my savings. An aunt and uncle, too, so I could decorate with more than movie posters. That's all."

Galen wasn't sure why, but the details of Michael's home and family intrigued him. He wanted to know more.

"You're welcome to come in for coffee," Michael said. He appeared to read Galen's mind. "It's the least I can do."

Georgie. Vons. Parmesan. It came back to him. *For the one he loved.* No longer for his stomach. His stomach was heavy with something else.

"I'd better not. Besides, that'd be pretty shifty on my part, putting you in a jam just to come to the rescue for a coffee reward. We cops love our coffee, but…." He chuckled.

Michael chuckled, too. "Okay. Don't say I didn't try."

Michael started to get out of the car but hesitated.

"Who's the best person in your department to talk to about some things I've observed in my travels around downtown? Nothing official. I just want to discuss some concerns and go from there."

"You can talk to me, if that's not too much of a reminder of a bad time." Galen hoped he covered well that he wanted to stay in touch with Michael.

Michael contemplated Galen. "No, that'd be okay."

Galen pulled out his phone. "I'm not trying to be a jerk. I'm serious as I say this. If you're okay with having your number in my phone, you can give it to me, and I'll text you, so we'll have each other's contact information."

"No, I'm okay with you having the number." Michael gave Galen his phone number, and Galen sent him a text.

"I know your phone's dead," Galen said, "and I hate to even say out loud that I remember why it died."

Michael smiled. "No worries." He hopped out of the car. "Take it easy," he said through the open door, with his hand on the outside door handle.

"You, too."

"Drive carefully." He still held open the door.

"I will. And, Michael?"

"Yes?"

"Shame on me. We drove all this way, and I even chit-chatted around it just now, but I never apologized, not in earnest."

They stared at each other.

"I'm really sorry I jammed you up tonight. And everybody else, too, who missed you because of me. I'm very sorry."

Michael smiled warmly. "Apology accepted, Galen."

I like how you say my name.

Michael shut the car door and headed for his front door. Galen watched for a moment longer than he needed to. He waved awkwardly, as a cover, as Michael glanced back at him and then punched four numbers into a small panel near the large, old-fashioned front door. To Galen, it looked like two-three-four-five.

He laughed a little, charmed by a very successful group of people keeping it simple, and backed out of the driveway.

The minute he was back on the road, he called Georgie, who hadn't called him because she was used to Galen's derailed exits from work and probably assumed he was tied up at a crime scene somewhere. That was when she had told him she would eat without him and the parmesan cheese. And Galen had gone for a longer drive, living to the fullest the fate he had sealed for himself.

Three hours after he had planned to be home, he finally walked through his front door. Georgie was asleep.

He ate microwaved leftovers and joined his wife in bed. She stirred but didn't wake up. He was relieved. He didn't understand why he had broken his date with Georgie for a man he had thrown in jail. He wasn't ready to explain himself, to her or to the atmosphere they fought in, to the heaviness of home and the enclosed room. And he wasn't in the mood for make-up sex when the fight was over.

He kissed her cheek and rolled onto his back. His thoughts returned to one thing—the same subject he thought about for every mile of his drive home—until he fell asleep.

Michael.

∞ Chapter 3 ∞

SIXTEEN

GALEN WISHED HE COULD AVOID the uncomfortable conversation with Georgie, but if he wanted to leave the house and spend the one day they both had free doing something that didn't include her, that conversation was his ticket out the door.

She worked odd hours at her hospital, but she had been a nurse there for eleven years, since college, and she hadn't worked on Sundays for ages.

Galen had similar Sunday privileges in his job. Since they had been married, they had dated on Sundays. Often, their first two activities were breakfast and a seduction, of one by the other, with the morning spent in bed. It was awkward explaining to her that on that Sunday, he had other plans.

"It's just this once."

She had just stepped out of the shower. He had always appreciated how her sinewy body had given her an alluring androgynous look. When they made love, he touched her everywhere to feel her incredible firmness. He enjoyed embracing her as they took it to the heights, and he often couldn't get there without his hands somewhere on her tight, lean body. But that morning, the sight of her nakedness couldn't keep him home.

"For, who was it, again?" she said. "Some guy you arrested?"

Her brown hair tumbled in a carefree but not careless way around her shoulders. She was textbook pretty, and her eyes shot out brilliance and wisdom whether she was furious, happy, sleepy, pensive, or scared. Arguments with her often went her way because she rested her position on logic. It was hard to beat, especially if a person just wanted what they wanted and had no good reason.

Galen resolved to win the argument that would let him leave the house by himself, even though he wanted what he wanted and had no good reason. *Michael*, with nothing beyond that word, the name, the man, came to mind. *Michael* was all, but it was enough.

"Yes, like I said. I rounded him up when I probably shouldn't have, and I'd like to make amends. He was trying to help people, and I screwed it up. Not good for a cop. He could have filed a complaint and didn't. I need to massage that some."

Michael had no intention of filing a complaint against Galen. Eight days had passed since Galen had arrested him, and they had talked or texted every day. Galen had unintentionally already massaged the situation.

It had started as a text from Michael the day after the arrest that made Galen's stomach tumble pleasantly. It was just two words: *Thank you.* But the simplicity of it felt familiar and intimate to Galen, as though they needed no extra talk between them, no wind-up or introduction or context.

He still hadn't understood why—he figured it was the same strange familiarity he felt the night of the arrest drawing him in— but it had excited him in a way he had never experienced. He felt a little high having his own connection with Michael that had nothing to do with the police department. He had texted back, *My pleasure.*

Later that day, Michael had e-mailed about a community meeting he hoped to hold outdoors, and he asked a few questions about police presence.

Galen called the following day to give Michael a friendly reminder about some of the laws regarding distributing over-the-counter medicines to the public. While they were on the phone, they talked about work and told each other bad jokes, a new side of Galen he was trying out, and laughed easily.

The next day, Michael called Galen "to see if any street closures were planned" for a possible protest that might happen downtown, and that led to another long conversation. Galen had parked his patrol car away from the grid and spent over two hours on the phone with Michael.

They talked every day after that, sometimes following up with funny texts. And Galen had texted, *You should really talk to your neighbors and agree on a code that's a little harder to crack than 2-3-4-5.*

How did you know? Michael texted. He added an emoji of a baffled face with a finger that tapped its chin.

Cops. We have our ways, Galen texted. He inserted a smiling emoji that winked.

On Saturday, Michael called Galen and invited him to an outreach event happening Sunday. Galen had agreed without checking with Georgie, in a repeat of the parmesan cheese scandal, knowing he would have to explain himself to her.

Sunday had arrived, and Galen rose early. He flipped the order of things and showered before breakfast. He had taken extra time with his routine and told himself it was because he would be with a bunch of Michael's acquaintances, and he wanted to make a good impression. But as with the night he drove Michael home, he didn't buy his own explanation. He had no idea what could be going on other than a deep desire to impress Michael as part of a new bromance, but he sensed something was different.

Georgie did too.

"If I didn't know any better, I'd swear you had a crush on this guy, but I do know better, so I don't get it." She had taken her time getting dressed, first rubbing lotion on herself. As she often did, she handed Galen the bottle and aimed her back at him.

He glanced at her sleekness in the mirror and poured some lotion into his hands and returned the bottle to her. He applied the lotion up and down her back. When he got near the top of her buttocks, he performed a familiar tease and inched his way down each side of her bottom, taking care to squeeze the firm muscles there, to show her how much he admired the beauty of her body. None of it, not her naked front or her smooth back or her tight, beautiful behind, had been enough to entice him to undress for her and stay home.

"I just want to put the finishing touches on making amends. A day in my civvies, reaching out to the community, is a great thing for a cop and his career. How can a nurse not want to see people get the stuff they need?" That was his ace, and he played it.

She softened. "All right. But let's go someplace for dinner." She faced him and put her arms around him. Her taut breasts touched his shirt.

He returned the waist-hug and smiled. The top of her head just reached his chin, and he bent a little and kissed her forehead. While his hands were close to her naked bottom, he caressed it. "I promise, I'll get these obligations out of the way, and then it's dinner wherever you say." He patted her bottom with a light touch. "I'll be home early enough to shower and get clean for my girl." He genuinely liked her and enjoyed being near her and leaned in for a kiss.

"Okay. Okay. Just don't get too cozy with people out there. You know how people feel about cops."

"I won't. Don't worry." He gave her another quick kiss and left her there, still nude, to gather his wallet and keys and bolt out the door. He felt like he was sixteen and his parents had just loaned him the car to hang out with guys whose circles he had tried to break into all school year and who had finally invited Galen to join their fun. He didn't understand it.

∞

Galen arrived at Michael's small West Hollywood office and was nervous. The office was in an old-fashioned but pristine one-story building, with glass doors that led directly onto the street. Galen checked himself out in his reflection. Good or bad, it was too late. He opened the door and went in.

"Hi," Michael said. He lit up the minute Galen walked through the door. The upbeat reception flattered Galen. His stomach responded like it had the entire week when he had had any contact with Michael. It did a flip, a stronger one than usual because it was the first time he had seen Michael since the night he drove him home, and a thrill coursed through him.

He had expected a room full of volunteers, the way Michael had described it, but, besides Michael, there were just three other men.

"Hey!" Galen said. He thought he sounded dumb. "So, sign me up!" *Even dumber.* "Where do you want me?"

Michael laughed. "Ha, ha. You have to be careful around here asking that."

It took Galen a moment to get his own joke, but he soon laughed too. And his stomach did another flip, even as he still felt a little dumb. Somehow, though, he experienced a thrill at the implications that the other men in the room may feel some attraction to him. He assumed it was that thing between men where they enjoyed causing envy in others. He thought maybe any attraction to him meant he "had" something appealing about him. He wasn't sure, though.

Michael made introductions, and the other volunteers gathered around another staff person.

"Sunday's our hardest day," Michael said. "Most of the other organizations are closed, so we get more requests, more people stopping us, asking questions, needing things. It's gonna be a long day."

"Uh…about that. If I want to stay married," he chuckled, "I'll need to cut it by four-thirty."

Galen caught a flash of disappointment in Michael's face, but he seemed to recover quickly. "No worries. With the extra person—meaning you—we can cover more ground." He smiled as though it was not a problem. "But, one other thing…."

"Yep."

"If we run into any difficulties, it's better if you don't identify as a cop, uh, police officer. If these people think I've brought law enforcement down on them, they'll never trust me again."

"Not a problem. Cops are people too. We look the other way more than you know. Especially on our days off." He smiled.

Michael grinned a little wickedly. "Okay," he nodded. "It's not that I want you to pretend to be something you're not. It's just long-term planning I'm thinking about. Gotta keep my bridges intact."

"No. I get it." Galen became uneasy when Michael talked about his pretending to be something he wasn't. It felt like a reminder of something that hadn't happened, as though it portended a darker event. After a moment, the feeling passed, and he and Michael left.

They got on well in the field. Galen was used to talking to strangers, herding crowds, keeping order, using calm tones with distressed people, and gathering information in a way that made it seem like he wasn't. He also had Michael's stamina for walking long distances, and they each knew different crannies of the city so that they helped each other take shortcuts. Galen showed Michael entire homeless encampments he was unaware of that Galen knew of from his patrols and helped Michael broaden his reach.

Michael was ecstatic. They worked well together, and the time flew.

Three hours later, they had talked to over a hundred people and gathered a shopping list. Galen was surprised by how many people made no requests. They mostly just vented about how wrong life was or complained about people around them who bothered them. Almost everyone had choice words about the police.

The first time one let loose with a tirade about "asshole cops," Michael shot him a nervous look that said, "This isn't going to escalate, is it?" Galen winked and shook his head and grinned at the person and listened.

He did the same thing the next twenty, or so, times and was amazed he gathered valuable insights between the name-calling and the vilification. A couple of times, he ginned up the negative talk, himself, to draw people out. There were five or six things he planned to do differently the next time he patrolled, based on some of the rants he heard.

Michael kept track of who wanted what by jotting down their location, so that the list read, RONNIE; TOOTHPASTE; CORNER OF SIXTH AND MAIN, and so forth.

By one o'clock, they were back from the store and handed out everything from shaving cream to chewing gum to writing utensils to condoms. By three-thirty, they had returned to Michael's office. The other staff and volunteers were still out, and they had the entire space to themselves. They fell into one of their easy conversations. Galen never wanted the day to end.

But it did.

At four-thirty, he got up to leave. That time, Michael expressed his disappointment. "Wish you could stay," he said.

"Me, too."

"You were just getting comfortable with the routine around here."

"I know, but duty calls."

Michael let out a little puff through his nose that wasn't quite laughter and that hid an opinion he kept to himself.

"What?"

"Nothing."

"No, there's something."

"Well, you said, 'Duty.' Is that how you see your marriage? As a duty?" His eyes met Galen's.

Galen was flustered. He wanted to dodge the question, but he gave an honest answer. "Maybe. I mean, when you pledge your life, you carry through, right?"

"Carry through? If that's how you see it, sure. And if you made the right pledge."

Galen's stomach did a different kind of flip. He felt punched in the gut by a truth, one he didn't understand, like a vague fact that hid itself from him, a memory he could almost recall but that he couldn't bring to the fore of his mind.

"How can anyone be sure they made the right pledge?" But even as he asked the question, he heard the equivocation in his logic.

"Well, for starters, you don't wonder whether you're sure." Michael had heard the equivocation, too. "You don't think of it as a duty. You relish it, embrace it, love it, like you hopefully love the person." He hesitated, then said, "And you don't ponder out loud about wishing you had people around you who had your back, who knew you coming and going and needed you around because of who you were and didn't treat you like you were incidental."

He had parroted back Galen's exact words about how he felt moving around between different relatives after his parents died.

How did you remember that?

"Not meaning at all to be insensitive, and really just being a friend who heard you that night in the car and wonders right now, for your sake. Really, Galen. In fact, I'm sorry if I shouldn't have said that. I guess I can't unknow that about you. I'm sorry if it's wrong to bring it up."

They were both quiet. As Galen had expressed those feelings that night on the ride home, he had thought he had talked about a time much earlier in his life, but he realized he had made a slip possibly of the Freudian kind and given the impression he felt that way in the present.

He floundered. "You're okay. It's okay. I know how you meant it, and I'm the one who ran my mouth that night, and you were kind enough to listen. I'm grateful for that."

Which makes your question worse. You really want to know why I feel a duty to someone who doesn't make me feel surrounded by love.

"Really, we can drop it."

"No, it's okay. I mean, I love Georgie. I do. And she loves me." He looked away and thought about how to continue. "I guess we've just fallen into our patterns, you know? We've set up certain expectations, and we follow through, is all, and meet at the designated time, you know? Marriage isn't one, big romance. Sometimes, it's just grocery shopping or a ride to the dentist, as friends."

"Look, it's none of my business. Far be it from me to judge a man for going home to his wife." He shifted some items on the desk in front of him that needed no shifting.

"What just happened? Are you angry with me?"

"No, no. Listen, no. Not at all. Maybe just a little jealous." He bit his top lip and waited to see how that landed with Galen.

Galen didn't say anything.

"Jealous that our conversation is over, and I have no control over it." He smiled without showing his teeth. It was a slightly sad, resolute smile. "No worries." He moved a stapler back to where it had been before and laughed a little. "I'll get over it."

"Well, for what it's worth, I wish we'd had more time to do the post-mortem on the day."

"There's always next time."

"Except, if my wife has the day off, I'll probably have to skip the next time." He laughed it off, but he thought he sounded artificial.

And it bothered him that he would miss more Sunday outings with Michael.

Michael offered his hand. "Then I should thank you for coming out this time."

Galen ignored Michael's hand. "You sound like you're saying goodbye."

"Aren't I?" Michael dropped his hand. His tone had an edge.

"Now, I *am* offended. No, you're not saying goodbye. I'll see you. Soon." He turned and headed for the door.

"Galen," Michael said. His voice traveled easily over the room empty of people. Galen stopped and turned back to look at Michael. "I hope so. I'm looking forward to it," Michael said.

Galen took a moment to respond. "Me, too," he finally said.

He barely turned again to leave, and Michael said, "Galen."

Galen looked at him. "Yes?"

"Do you ever...regret it? Pulling your mother's file?"

Galen's eyebrows went up, and he blinked several times.

He was stunned. Not even his last therapist, the one he needed after he pulled the file and learned of the horrors, had asked him that. He knew she had been too afraid to send Galen over the edge. She had taught him to live with his choice, instead, and to see that step he had taken as progress.

He glanced across the room at nothing and remembered the photos, the wicked way his mother's expression had settled into a half smile, the upturned furniture in the background that indicated a physical fight, the sun coming through the windows on a Sunday morning. Despite those images, his answer would always be the same.

"No." He stared at the ground and swallowed hard. "This may make no sense," and he looked at Michael and was taken aback by the compassion on his face, "but my dad didn't die alone. My mom was there." He took a deep breath. "Looking at those pictures…well, somebody had to let my mom talk, to a loved one, about what happened to her." He looked away again and saw in his mind the sun, once more, coming through their living room window, and he looked at Michael. "Those photos were how she told her story. The last people she spoke to were her killers. She deserved to have someone who loved her erase that and let her say, 'I got hurt. Look what they did to me.' She wouldn't have wanted it to be me who did it, but she needed someone. Who else could do it? She was always there for me. We were family. I loved her. Still do. It was the least I could do."

Michael took a step forward. "I'm sorry I brought it up. I'm an asshole."

"No, you're a friend. You're the only person I've ever told the other reason, besides the just needing to know, why I looked and put myself through that."

"I…I'm sorry."

"Don't be." He touched Michael's arm. "Thanks." And he left.

Before the door closed behind him all the way, he heard one word.

"Shit," Michael had said.

∞ Chapter 4 ∞

SIDEWALKS AND STREETLIGHTS

GALEN CLOCKED JUST ENOUGH TIME at home. He was available to Georgie more than he was away from her, but his marriage began to sag, right in the middle of its foundation—where trust lay—as he found more excuses and told more white lies to spend time with Michael.

A week after his first Sunday with Michael, Galen had done what he had sworn he wouldn't do and asked Georgie for understanding for one more Sunday. That day, he spent twelve hours with Michael, covering every inch of his route with him and taking an empty desk in his office at the end of their long day together to help him type up field reports.

Gradually, he expanded his involvement to occasional weeknights at Michael's office, after work, when Georgie worked late, ostensibly to receive or provide updates and make suggestions he could have easily made through e-mail or over the phone.

He hadn't meant to scheme but a convenient plot had unfolded. He had contacted Michael for big and small things and sometimes spent just five or ten minutes with him so that no matter how or when he got in touch, it was normal for them.

He needed that, more than he understood. He only knew that he was attached to Michael in a way that demanded more than the casual, informal contact he had with his other friends.

It didn't take long for Michael to move beyond the realm of his office and invite Galen to his apartment. After the first few visits there, Michael gave Galen full and free use of the two-three-four-five code for the building's front door.

Galen lied—to himself and to Georgie—about why he spent time with Michael, but he still hadn't figured out what the truth was.

He didn't know how to define the new need in his life, why it was there or about whom it was—Michael or Georgie or himself.

He had sex with Georgie on a regular basis, good sex, but Michael captivated him, and he wondered, fleetingly, about kissing him, thoughts that had mystified him but thrilled him, too. Sometimes, Michael's face came to Galen at the height of sex with Georgie, in an instant that lasted no longer than a flash—the first few times. Over time, he had enjoyed the combination of climaxing and Michael's face so much that, gradually, he let Michael infiltrate his mind for long stretches of his lovemaking with Georgie and told himself it was the newness of the connection and their friendship and somehow missing Michael when he wasn't there that intoxicated him and preoccupied his mind. After a while, those thoughts travelled with him outside the bedroom and distracted him from work.

He patrolled on a dull Tuesday night while Georgie worked at the hospital and tamped down thoughts of Michael and sex and Georgie and kept his eyes alert.

As though Michael read his mind and subconsciously answered Galen's mental calls, Galen's phone rang.

A caller ID photo he had taken of Michael talking to a friend on the street appeared in the display. Galen had wanted to use a closeup of Michael he had stolen on the second Sunday they had canvassed together. They had stopped to rest on a bench in Grand Park, the same park in the middle of downtown where Galen had arrested Michael. Michael had leaned his head back and closed his eyes. The sun had shone on his face in a way that made him look striking yet not out of reach. He was stunning, but he appeared emotionally available. Galen had snapped the photo and frozen Michael's vulnerability in one picture. The closed eyes hinted at a person in the throes of quiet passion, but the setting was chaste.

Galen loved the picture, but he thought it better not to use it as Michael's caller ID photo. If Georgie happened to see his phone ring when Michael called, she would wonder why her husband had a photo of a man who appeared to strike a "sexy" pose flashing at him when that man called. Galen wasn't sure of the answer. To be safe, he had gone with the more neutral photo of Michael engaged in a platonic conversation.

"Hello." Galen's mood spiked.

"It's me," Michael had said. Not, "It's Michael," the way friends did, Galen noticed, but, "It's me," the way lovers and intimates did.

"Hi."

"Just a quick question."

"Sure."

"Do you wear a vest?"

"You mean like a bullet-proof vest?"

"Yeah. I've only seen you in uniform once, the night you picked me up. I can't remember if you were wearing a vest, and I don't recall you mentioning whether you wear one."

Galen's stomach did a familiar flip. "Yeah, I wear a vest."

"All the time? On patrol, I mean?"

Galen's mouth was right on the phone. "Yeah."

He heard Michael breathe a little sigh.

"Okay," Michael said. "Good," he said. And after a while, "Bye."

"Bye."

Galen found the other photo of Michael in his phone and stared at it for a long time after he hung up.

∞

Five days later, Galen and Georgie were at a barbecue at Georgie's sister Tracy's house. Michael and the stranger on the street appeared in Galen's phone. He silenced it without answering and for the next several hours barely paid attention to anything anyone said. He wondered what Michael had wanted and what he had missed by not taking the call.

Eventually, the beer and soda he had drunk helped him. He excused himself to use the bathroom and texted Michael.

Sorry I missed your call, he typed. He hoped Michael was near his phone. There was only so long he could stand around in a bathroom waiting for a return text, but his phone lit up almost immediately.

No worries. Sunday. Busy day, I know. I was just going to see what you were up to tomorrow night.

Same old, Galen texted. *Dinner alone at home. Work ends at 7:00. Georgie's got a late shift.*

Are you up for dinner *not* alone? With some friends of mine? No stress. They do a lot of their own outreach. I thought they'd like to meet a friendly police officer (not cop—I know better), and, there, he had inserted smiling-face and police-officer emojis, *who could give them law enforcement's perspective.*

Formal? Informal?

Downright raggedy, he texted, with a clown emoji. *Anything better than jeans is an insult.*

Would you like me to bring anything?

Just yourself. After work? I'll move the time for sitting down to eat to 7:45 or 8:00. Can you make it?

Galen caught himself in the bathroom mirror grinning hard enough for it to hurt.

I'll be there. He inserted a smiling face wearing sunglasses and added a wine-glasses-toasting-each-other emoji.

Fantastic. I can't wait.

Neither can I.

∞

Galen got along well with Michael's friends. He fit in better with Michael's people than he did with many of his cop friends or Georgie's family.

There were five men, besides Michael. They were all openly gay. Two were in a couple, and the other three were single. The seven men gelled well at dinner. Conversations and laughter flowed. After the party had moved to the living room and everyone sat around informally, Galen fought with himself not to stare when the couple occasionally kissed, but he was sucked into their dynamic.

His status as a straight man, in Michael's apartment with his friends, made him feel strange. He never brought up Georgie or his married life and found ways to talk around it all evening. To closet himself, he stuck to work and homelessness and the pitfalls to outreach and hoped no one asked him head-on about his married life.

His job helped him hide. He almost never wore his wedding ring because he didn't want criminals to know he had a spouse whose life they could use to threaten him. After what happened with his parents, it was important to him that he not reveal too much of who he was to perpetrators. The ring stayed locked up at home unless he and Georgie spent time with her family. There wasn't even a tan line on his hand.

He thought he did a good job of blending in by the time the party broke up. They all exchanged contact information, and Galen took a group shot to use as the picture in his cell phone that would appear if any of them called him.

He beat Georgie home and felt compelled to take a shower. He couldn't remember, but he thought he had let Michael and a couple of the other men get close to him, and he worried he had picked up their scents on his own clothing. That wouldn't bother Georgie, but to Galen's senses, the smells were powerful and intoxicating and made him seem guilty of something.

When Georgie got home, she took the shower she always did after a day at the hospital. When she stepped out, that time, he let her nudity seduce him into a late evening of sex.

A feeling of a lack of fulfillment hovered over him. It had been there since he had left Michael's. It made him hungry for the sex. He tried, out of guilt for his evening at Michael's, to stop Michael's face from flashing in front him while he rocked along with Georgie, but Michael was there.

Galen touched Georgie's lean thighs and small, small breasts, but he saw Michael. And he rocked harder and moved faster than usual, excited by who else was in his bed.

Usually, no matter what went through his mind, something about Georgie took him to the heights, but that night, Michael's face and the remnants of his scent that traveled around Galen's memory sent him over the edge of ecstasy. As he finished, he stopped himself from crying out Michael's name, in relief and gratitude for his being there, in some way.

Rather than feel guilty, he felt liberated by the fantasy. He couldn't wait to make love to Michael's image again.

And he knew his marriage was in real trouble.

∞

Chet wondered about Galen's marriage, too, and like Galen, he focused on Michael's peculiar presence in it. At first, he had joked that Galen arrested perps to gain friends. Then one day, he cornered Galen in the locker room, when he was sure they were alone.

"Are you and Georgie doing okay?"

"Yeah. Why do you ask? And by that, I mean why do you ask what's none of your business?" Chet was his best friend and hadn't warranted such a rude response, but Galen had no good answers, for himself, even, so he hid behind an overblown desire for privacy, to turn Chet away from nosiness.

"It *is* my business. You and Georgie are both my friends."

"And?"

"It seems like you're letting some new weird friendship hijack your life."

The word "weird" bothered Galen. "I'm not weird."

But he wondered if he was queer. He didn't think he was gay, at least not sexually, but he was unsure how he was wired emotionally. He thought wanting a deeper connection to Michael might have been why he saw his face during sex with Georgie.

Chet had left Galen in the locker room to stew in his own juices.

That night, at home, Galen turned to the Internet for answers.

For several more days, he read blogs and spied on forums where people chatted about queer life.

He found terrifying answers. And thrilling ones that he was sure would tear a rent down the middle of his life.

∞

Galen went through his workdays distracted, by Michael, Chet's reaction to Michael, and his life with Georgie and the hour-by-hour debate he had with himself about her and who he was beginning to think he was.

That distracted way of life was how he had almost been blown to pieces on patrol.

He had responded, along with several other units and the fire department, to a call about a gas leak. The area needed to be cleared of bystanders, and it was the job of the police to do the clearing.

Firefighters in full safety gear approached a manhole cover, the first window into the leak, with caution, but Galen casually strolled near their vicinity, wearing just his vest.

Just as the firefighters were within steps of the manhole cover, the leak was pushed beyond its limits.

Something underground exploded.

The manhole cover, and several square feet of blacktop that surrounded it, blew up and caved in at the same time.

Galen had been just outside the circle of destruction. The ground beneath him had stayed intact during the blast, but the reverberations were powerful. They knocked him to his feet.

On his way down, he caught sight of three firefighters the explosion had tossed high landing hard on the asphalt.

Years on the force told Galen one of them died on impact. The other two lay in the street, motionless but able to moan.

Galen had been far enough away to avoid a similar fate. He stood up on his own and staggered out of the way of the chaos. He shook off the shock and stepped back into the confusion to help.

His plan hit a wall. Someone ordered him to go to the hospital in an ambulance. Hidden injuries, they said.

He dodged a second blast of a different sort when they sent him to a hospital that was not where Georgie worked.

He received a third lucky charm when the doctors let him leave with a headache and cleared him to return to work that day. He had fallen and gotten up, and there was no reason he couldn't work. His biggest irritation was waiting for a ride back to his car, which he'd left at the blast site, and being told once he got there to return to home base to fill out paperwork.

Back at the station, he wished he had been told to go home.

Michael waited for him in the lobby area.

The hairs on Galen's neck stood up. His ears became hot with the rush of blood his feelings sent there. He understood his reaction and felt ashamed: He feared Michael's presence in the station would expose a side of himself he wasn't ready for people to see.

"Uh, I can't talk, right now," Galen said.

"I'm just glad you can talk at all. I heard about the blast. It's all over the news. They're saying two are dead and one is fighting to stay alive."

Galen shifted on his feet. He feigned nonchalance. He wanted Michael to leave. "That's right."

"I tried to call you, but your phone is going straight to voice mail."

"Yeah, I was…somewhere where I was required to shut it down. I forgot to turn it back on." He pulled out his phone and turned it on and noticed six missed calls from Michael. There were three texts, too.

And three calls from Georgie. In his quest to get right back to work, he had forgotten about his phone, and because they had ushered him past the waiting room right into an examination room at his hospital, he hadn't seen a television, which would have reminded him Georgie would see the news on a television in a waiting room at her hospital and be scared for Galen. He really needed Michael to leave.

"I showed up here to see how you were and someone said you were at the scene?" It was a question and an accusation, as though Galen shouldn't have been at the scene and owed Michael an explanation.

"Yeah, I was there. It's my job. But I'm fine."

Michael shook his head. "Cops. You could have been killed. Don't you care?"

"I do, but I have to do the job." His eyes darted around the station. "Look, uh, you should probably go."

"Why? This police station belongs to the public. Anyone should be able to walk in here. Lord knows I got dragged in here."

"I said I was sorry about that."

Michael shook his head and sighed.

"That's not what I meant. I just meant that these people should be the last ones to care that I'm here. I wanted to know that you were okay. Is that a problem?"

"It is here."

Michael's face changed.

"Ahh. I see. No gay friends in the station, is that it?"

Galen was insulted but he kept his temper in check.

"You know that's not what I mean. I just mean that my wife is a nurse. Like you, she's probably heard the news. I missed her calls with yours, and she may already be on her way here to check on me. And I'm at work, and I have to get back to the job."

"But she can be here, while you do the job. And, more important, if she's here, I can't be? To check on a friend? Ask yourself why that is, Galen."

"Look, all—"

"Save it."

He left.

∞

Things had been awkward between Galen and Michael since the day of the explosion. They texted and talked a few times, stilted conversations, and Michael had made excuses for why he didn't need Galen's help with outreach efforts.

Galen regretted that he had rejected Michael's concern. Without meaning to, he had relegated him to casual nosy bystander status and treated him like an outsider.

The truth had been that when the blast threw Galen to the ground, the first person he thought of was Michael. Many of his sensibilities centered around what Michael thought or would think about something, where Michael was, whether Michael would like a song Galen heard on the radio or the food in a restaurant where Galen ate, when he would see Michael again and what they would talk about and do when it happened.

The new wedge that had settled between them, made of what, Galen didn't know—maybe resentment, disdain for Galen's life with Georgie, subconscious punishment for what looked a lot like homophobia from Galen—made him miserable.

For the third week in a row, he spent his Sunday with Georgie. They had gone to Zuma Beach with a picnic and mixed moods. Hers was upbeat. The issue of Michael had seemed to have gone away. She no longer competed with him for Galen's free time. To Georgie, it appeared that her husband's man-crush on a new friend had waned the way the energy in most new friendships tended to do once the freshness wore off.

Galen knew it was far different from that. It felt to him as though he and Michael had broken up. His mood at the beach was polite but disconnected. He and Georgie rode boogie boards and napped on blankets and helped each other with sunscreen, but Galen had no deep need to be there with Georgie. They got along fine, but that was because, other than a prickliness about Michael and schedules and Sundays, there existed no real conflicts between them, although in the weeks since the explosion, a topic had crawled out of the wreckage and agitated them more than usual.

Georgie had pushed again about having a child. Any time before the explosion that the subject had come up, she had always been able to drop it if Galen said he wasn't ready for kids.

Hopeful for the same result, he balked again. He was thirty-three and she was thirty-one, and they had plenty of time to become parents, he had argued.

That time, though, Georgie countered with toughness. She said she was afraid to lose Galen to an on-duty tragedy and that she wanted his child in the event something awful happened. She had made it sound tragic and romantic and as though he would be denying their unborn child his or her destiny if he didn't agree, and, yet, at first, he didn't agree, not enough to surrender and begin a family. If he really could die young, he didn't want to leave a child without a parent the way fate had left him without parents.

And then he thought about his mother and father and their legacy and how he was just as likely to live a long life as he was to die in the line of duty, and he wondered if he shouldn't try to have a child with Georgie and somehow rebuild what was lost. The idea that he might have a son or daughter that carried on bits of his parents lured him in a little.

They were at an impasse that was, for the moment, mostly polite. They were still great friends. If they weren't debating whether to start a family, and if Michael's name didn't come up, neither did any problems. Georgie spent a romantic day at the beach with her husband. Galen hung out with his wife, anxious to reconnect with Michael. He had run out of ideas for how to regain ground with Michael.

The day before, Saturday, he had texted Michael an offer to stop by with supplies for the Sunday outreach, but Michael turned him down. He did so with a bonus dig at Galen. At least that was how Galen took it. *That's okay,* Michael had texted. *Paul's on tap to help, and he's free into the evening. Late summer nights mean more time outside and more time on duty. We'll be okay. Thanks, though.*

Galen wondered who the hell Paul was and what "free into the evening" on a "late summer night" meant. The text bothered him into *his* night on Saturday and Sunday at the beach, even when waves tossed him around and he had to regain his bearings with saltwater in his eyes and seaweed tangled in his legs. Even then, Michael's veiled references to time spent with someone else dominated Galen's thoughts.

Galen and Georgie left the beach before dark. By the time they got home, unpacked their paraphernalia, and showered, Galen was despondent.

He knew of only one way to camouflage his longing to be elsewhere. He seduced his wife and had sex with her until neither of them could walk. He saw Michael's face the entire time. He shouted Michael's name in his head, and it echoed around his mind with every throb as he came, again and again.

Georgie fell asleep wearing a slight grin, but Galen lay awake and tried to envision who Paul was, what he looked like, and whether he, Galen, had seen him on an earlier Sunday.

He remembered nothing and no one. He filled in the missing pieces with his imagination and came up with a rugged sensitivity and winning smile and sense of humor that landed every joke with style.

The next day, he texted Michael from work. Michael didn't text back. On Tuesday, he left Michael a voice mail that went unreturned. He saw himself behaving like a clingy boyfriend and spent the following two days buried in his job. On Thursday night, he and Georgie went to an all-you-can-eat happy hour with Chet and his girlfriend Brianna.

By Friday, Galen hadn't heard from Michael. It was the first time a week had gone by without contact.

Even though Michael had rejected his efforts to volunteer, Galen tried one more time to use that to gain access.

He went to Michael's office at the end of his shift on Friday. Michael greeted him with indifference.

"Hi!" Galen had said. He thought he sounded dumb again.

"Hi," Michael said. "Uh, did we have an appointment?"

"No. I just hadn't heard how things were going and thought I'd stop by."

"Well, I'm headed out. This is not a good time. I know you understand about not showing up where people work. And unlike the police station, this is not a public space. It's a private foundation."

The rebuke and the rebuff stung. Worse, Michael barely looked at him. He seemed to be in a hurry. He stood over a computer and clicked the mouse several times to close files and windows.

"That's okay," Galen said. He acted like Michael hadn't basically told him he would like him to leave. "I can head out with you. Maybe we can grab a bite?"

"That's not really going to work," Michael said. "I've got a date." He still didn't look at Galen. Instead, he tidied some papers on the desk.

"A date?"

"Yeah, you know, when two people who enjoy being around each other get together to be around each other?" He looked at Galen.

"I know what a date is. I've had a few of them."

"I know, like, with your wife? How is your wife, by the way?"

"Georgie's fine. She's also off-limits as a topic of discussion." His tone was more "police officer" than he had intended.

"Until you need to hide behind her."

"I don't hide behind my wife."

Michael chuckled. "Anyway…," he said. He tucked in the chair that was a little away from the desk and turned off the lights in the office. A streetlight shone through the glass doors.

"What does that even mean?" Galen said in the semi-dark.

"I'm locking up." Michael headed for the door. Galen followed him.

"Look. I didn't come here to argue with you."

"Well, I have other plans, so I clearly had no expectation of what would happen when you got here since I wasn't expecting you to be here."

"I know. You have a date. You said that already."

They were outside. Michael locked the office door and pulled down a large, metal gate that covered the façade to his office. He locked that, too.

The noise from the gate rolling down had made it impossible to continue conversation. Galen stood by, awkwardly, wondering whether he had been dismissed by the gate noise.

The sidewalk was mostly empty. An occasional pedestrian passed them without paying them much attention. Michael took a few steps from the office, and Galen followed him.

Michael stopped, and Galen stopped too.

Galen worked up the nerve to ask what had been on his mind, even as they bickered inside the office. Once the thought had entered his head, it was all he could think about. "Who's your date with?"

"None of your business."

"Paul?"

"What part of 'none of your business' did you not get?" He turned and walked down the street.

Galen didn't follow him that time. Instead, he stood under the streetlight and asked a question at full volume, that anyone also on the sidewalk could have heard.

"Are you fucking him?"

Michael turned and said, "Ex*cuse* me?"

They fought with thirty feet of sidewalk between them.

"You heard me. This Paul guy. Are you fucking him?"

"That is none of your goddamned business!"

"Maybe it is!"

"No, fucking your wife is your business. Who I fuck is mine!"

"So, you *are* screwing him!"

Michael walked up the sidewalk and stood one inch from Galen. "Who I screw or fuck or get down with is none of your business. You have no right showing up here expecting me to be so happy you dropped your nice little married life to come deign to see me."

"For your information, I didn't drop anything to come see you because I never picked it back up the night I let it go to take you home from jail."

Their faces were close, as they had been when Galen had confronted Michael in his jail cell. Neither of them moved. Galen became intoxicated by the sweet scent of Michael's breath and the proximity of his mouth, which Galen had inexplicably desired to kiss almost since the first time he had seen it.

"Do it," Michael said.

The words startled Galen, for he feared Michael had read his mind. "What are you talking about?"

"You know what I'm talking about. Do it." Michael's eyes taunted Galen. "Your wife and your cop buddies aren't here, now. You have no excuse not to."

Galen looked into Michael's eyes and fought with himself harder than he had about anything in a long time to keep from kissing Michael, for then it would be over, and it would also be the beginning, of what, he had no idea. A homosexual relationship between a heterosexual man who was homoromantic, *maybe*, and a gay man? An affair that led nowhere since he was married? A secret life from Georgie? A life without Georgie?

And *with* Michael.

He wanted that.

Without warning himself or Michael, he kissed Michael hard. The moment their mouths touched, he expected Michael to push him away and hit him, but instead he felt the unquestionable sensations of a mouth that responded. He took it as permission to go farther, to go all the way in. He opened his mouth and met Michael's tongue with his own.

They stood under the streetlight and kissed for what felt like forever to Galen. It was heaven. It was better than he imagined, richer, deeper, softer, sexier than he ever would have thought kissing another man would be. As if he had been born to kiss Michael, he brought his hands up and cradled Michael's face and let one hand slide through Michael's hair and rest on the back of his head. His hand played with Michael's hair in an easy rhythm that flowed with the rhythm of the kiss. Michael's upper body relaxed, and they settled into a long exchange of deep kisses.

I'm a married cop standing in the middle of the sidewalk kissing a man, and I don't ever want it to stop. I love it. I love—

Out of nowhere, Michael pulled away but immediately tipped his forehead onto Galen's and closed his eyes.

"This is bullshit, Galen." There was no anger in his tone, as there had been the night he had been arrested and had shouted those same words. It was simply what he thought.

Before Galen could respond, Michael walked away.

Galen stood under the streetlight and watched him go, still feeling Michael's lips on his and comparing the real-life kiss to the thousands he had dreamt of since he had met Michael. He finally narrowed down what he felt to one thought.

He's right. This is bullshit.

∞ Chapter 5 ∞

CONFESSIONS

THREE SUNDAYS HAD PASSED SINCE Galen had kissed Michael. They hadn't spoken since Michael left Galen under the streetlight on the sidewalk in front of his office.

Galen had reached out, but Michael refused him.

Let's talk, Galen had texted.

Michael responded, *Twice I've walked away from you, once at the police station and once after a kiss I don't understand. It's symbolic of where we're supposed to be—away from each other. Let it go.*

But Galen couldn't let Michael go.

For the first few days after their kiss, despite the distance between them, Galen had acted like a giddy teen who had discovered that the person he fantasized about liked him too, a feeling he had never had but had seen in others as a young man. He was happy Georgie was in his life, but he had never felt dizzy over her, the way he did about Michael.

He replayed the kiss in his mind incessantly. Addicted to the image of Michael's mouth on his, with Michael's face close to his, and the pleasure he had felt at his tongue touching Michael's, he took sustenance from that moment on the sidewalk to an obsessive extent. After four days, though, the buzz had worn off, and Galen was left with the misery and the melancholy of unrequited longings.

It drove him mad, and he sought answers.

He spent days again on the Internet trying to figure out who he was, which, in turn, forced him to look hard at his relationship with Georgie. Realizations that scared him, for they signaled that he had led the wrong life and would have to destroy Georgie's to get to the right one, would no longer be dismissed.

He finally saw that Georgie had been the only woman he had dated seriously.

He was sexually attracted to her because her lean, trim body with small breasts had a male essence to it.

The odd hours they worked released him from overlong periods of time spent with her.

The final truth was the hardest: He loved her dearly, like a friend, which made affection between them easy, but it had led to a mistake. It caused him to assume the affection must have followed romantic love, which wasn't true, and the assumption had masked that he wasn't *in* love with his wife. He only loved her.

Accepting that he wasn't in love with Georgie gave birth to many more questions. They had painful answers except for one.

He realized he had fallen into a life that was a lie, one that behaved like a mind in an altered state. On the one hand, he felt no overt sexual attraction to men, although there were subtle nuances to maleness that intrigued him, while the women he was drawn to weren't overly feminine, with severe curves and large breasts. On the other hand, that giddy, chemical, inexplicable feeling that came with romantic love was something he only had for men.

Of that he became sure.

He contemplated for hours, for days, really, the friendships he'd had with men over the years, and he realized he had been in love with three of them. Noah in high school was one of them. A young man in college named Robert who had gotten Galen through Cultural Anthropology with coffee and late nights studying and long conversations Galen looked forward to a week ahead of time was another.

The third was Michael.

The painful memories he had repressed all those years ago, about Noah and Robert, during those first four of five years of the aftermath of his parents' murders, returned to torment him and make him see the truth about the boy and the man he had loved long before.

That he loved Michael had been the only answer that hadn't hurt. It was the only truth that made him feel joyous and hopeful about his life, even if a life with Michael would represent the mirror of what he lived with Georgie. Instead of being with someone with whom sex had been easy without the right kind of love, he would be with someone he loved who didn't sexually attract him beyond kissing and being near one another. Galen preferred the second scenario, though, the one in which he was with Michael, for nothing that mattered to his happiness would be missing.

In his own way, he fantasized about Michael, about intimacy between them, as men in love. He could handle closeness and nudity and affection and kissing a man he was in love with, if they were together, as a couple. What he no longer wanted to do was live with and share himself with someone he loved in a nonromantic way.

He also respected Georgie too much to ask her to live a lie. She deserved to be with a person who loved her most, in relation to everyone and everything else, whose romantic love for her was so etched in his heart, he couldn't envision an existence that didn't include her. And Galen wanted a life that allowed him to be around Michael whenever he chose, to try for something, but what, Galen wasn't sure.

He saw no easy way. He had no easy out. Georgie wasn't the enemy. Galen was. He couldn't escape by using anger at her or righteousness about having been wronged in some way as an excuse.

And Michael wouldn't speak to him, and he saw no way to overcome that obstacle.

Galen refused to show up at Michael's office or his apartment without an invitation. Not only could he not face the blatant rejection, but he had to be careful. He was a police officer, and Michael had a right not to be harassed by the cops.

Not seeing Michael left Galen to wonder what Michael thought, how he felt about Galen.

It brought him back to their kiss.

Michael had given as good as he had gotten. It was Galen's first kiss with a man but not his first kiss, period, and he knew reciprocation when he felt it. Michael had not only returned the kiss, but he had helped choreograph it, had explored Galen's mouth with his own. He had made moves with his lips and tongue that had guided his half of the kiss to make it more enjoyable for himself and for them both. The kiss had blossomed and metamorphosed, as it went on under the streetlight, into many enjoyable versions of the initial coming together of their mouths. Afterward, when Michael had called the entire situation "bullshit", he hadn't been complaining, at least not entirely. He sounded as though he laid a problem at Galen's feet for him to solve.

Galen had taken the challenge, but he didn't see how he could find a solution if Michael wouldn't speak to him.

∞

Soon, Galen faced another mountain. He wanted to come out to Chet about being queer. He wasn't sure why. He may have needed Chet to know so that he lived a little less of a lie. Or, maybe he was hoping for acceptance from someone in the heterosexual world, a notion that bothered him. He could have even been hoping for a dry run of a conversation with Georgie that loomed. Or, he may have simply needed a little understanding from a friend. Whatever the reason, he wanted to tell Chet.

He had read online about different ways to come out and found out there were as many ways as there were people who came out. And for each person, coming out changed, depending upon who was getting the news. One person may come out twenty-eight different ways, and once a person lived "out", they would have to come out again and again and again, each time they explained their life to new people. *This is Bill, my husband. Yes, I'm gay*, he imagined was how it often went.

Too, he had wondered if he should bother to come out since his attraction to a certain type of female kept him well-cloaked. But he knew that no matter what happened with Michael, it was men he was naturally drawn to, and he no longer wished to hide that from himself or from anyone else.

He requested a work shift that overlapped Chet's and met him for lunch out of their patrol area in a small restaurant that had little traffic and no cops in it.

"I know you need your alone time with me, but seriously, this place is nowhere," Chet had joked.

Galen had taken the opening. He had thought he would be scared and dodge the issue until the server asked if they wanted to order dessert, but with nothing but their free tap water on the table, before they touched their menus, he dove right in and faced the fear.

"*You*, I can barely stand, but," he hesitated, nervous, "what if the same weren't true for a different man? A different man and me, I mean. Meaning a different man I could stand." He looked right at Chet, terrified of rejection.

Chet stared back, for a long while. He reached for a menu, and Galen tapped it down. "Don't." He pulled Chet into a long, expectant stare. "Don't, Chet, please. You're my best friend."

"And as your best friend, I gotta ask what you're drinking, or smoking, or whatever."

"Look, I get that you think I'm confused. And I am, or I was, in the other direction. I'm not living my truth because I've been baffled by who I am this whole time. I didn't get it either, at first.

But…," he said, and he let the word dangle. He hoped Chet would pick it up and help him say the hard words.

Chet raised his eyebrows, as if to ask, "What?" with impatience.

"Forget it. I can see that when the shit hits it, you're not my friend. Let's go." He started to get up to leave.

It was Chet's turn to block the action with a gentle hand to Galen's forearm. "Sit down." He looked Galen in the eye, and from his seated position, he appeared to be more beseeching. "Seriously. Sit down."

Galen sat down.

"Okay," Chet said. "Okay." After another moment, he said again, "Okay." Finally, he said, "Michael?"

"Yeah." Galen sighed. "I know it seems crazy, except I look back on my life, and it makes sense. And, *no*, I'm not into you." He gave a small, sad smile. "But I have been…," he looked around and lowered his voice, "in love with two other men in my life. Once in high school, which I thought was a bromance that faded when I moved to Denver. With my parents and everything, I sort of forgot him for a while. I moved back to L.A. for college, and he had left for Boston, and that was it."

"Until…? You said there were two."

Galen appreciated Chet. "My senior year of college. Someone named Robert. I figured it was admiration for a smart study partner—"

A server arrived at their table. Galen froze. He had timed his confession wrong. He hadn't expected to have to choose between ranch or bleu cheese dressing or mull over what the soup of the day was while telling his best friend about men in his past with whom he had been in love. He faltered and lost his courage.

Without looking at the menus, Chet said, "Two cheeseburgers, everything on them, whatever that ends up being, Swiss on one,

American on the other, two fries, two diet Cokes, no dessert, and you can bring the check with the food."

"Okay," the server said, with a big smile. "We can do that." She left their table.

"Noah in high school and Robert in college," Chet said.

"Man, you're the best," Galen said. He inhaled and exhaled. "Noah and Robert. And when I became separated from them by the changes of life, I was in real pain, especially the second time. With Noah, my parents' deaths clouded everything. I leaned into everything with anger and fear and loneliness. Robert, though. That was tough. After college, I didn't date for a long, long time, not until Georgie. I know now I was pining for…him."

"But…Georgie. Don't you guys…?"

"All the time. That's the thing. I find women attractive. At least I thought I did. Georgie's…hot. But if you think about it, even though she's all woman, there's a guy-ish look to her." He lowered his voice even more. "Her body is lean and hard." He looked around again. "No curves," he whispered.

Chet bobbed his head back and forth, mimicking moving scales and weighing that statement. Finally, he said, "True. She's pretty in that sleek, slim-girl way."

"And she has a man's name. I mean, don't get me wrong. I know gender is up here," he tapped his head, "and not up and down here," he gestured at his body. "I don't have her mixed up with men, like she's interchangeable. She's a woman, but she has a certain…masculine appeal." He drank some water. "And, it…you know, sex," he mouthed, "feels right with her *because of that*. Although, lately…." He shook his head and saw in his mind Michael's face in bed with him and Georgie. "It's probably TMI, but suffice it to say I've been distracted there too."

Chet nodded and said, "Mmmm," as if to say, "I'm beginning to see."

"And…I've only ever really enjoyed it…with *her*. Other women were interesting, but you know…."

"Well, then…. I don't get it."

"Believe me," he kept his voice low, "I've been up and down the Internet saying the same thing and looking for answers. Identity takes a lot of forms. I guess mine comes down to," he said, moving his lips with almost no sound coming out of his mouth, "enjoying a certain kind of hetero sex, but, you know, romantically, my prefix is 'homo'." It was the first time he had said it to anyone but himself.

He had come out.

Chet contemplated the table as if answers lay there and shook his head in wonder. "Wow," he said.

"I know," Galen said. He mastered a low, even whisper that only Chet could hear. "I'm telling you, it wasn't easy figuring it out, but now that I know, 'heterosexual, maybe bisexual, and homoromantic' sounds right to me, so far."

Chet matched his whisper. "So, you're not gay? Or you are gay? I'm still confused."

"Queer, for sure. Gay, maybe. Depends on whether it's defined by how one feels wired emotionally or how one feels wired sexually. If we're talking emotions, I'm gay. If not, I don't know. Maybe pansexual because of how I detach gender from my attraction to Georgie, sexually, but I don't feel that way broadly. I don't even think I'm bi, but I don't know. I'd have to finally, you know, try things out with—"

"I get it."

"—to see what's really going on with my attraction to Georgie. I wonder if she's the only woman I like. I mean, and this is *only between us* because we've been friends since rookie time, but under her clothes, she really is lean…and flat. Maybe she satisfies a true attraction to men."

"Wow." Chet shook his head again. After a moment, he asked, "Do you love Georgie?"

"Not the way I love him."

"Wow."

"Can you handle it?"

Chet was quiet for a long time.

"You know?" he finally said. "I can. It's hard to think of you and Georgie not being solid, but—"

"Or broken up?"

Chet raised his eyebrows. "Are you serious?"

"Yes."

"Are you sure that's a good idea?"

"She deserves better than me, and I can't keep living a lie."

"So, you'd leave her for some dude who's not even speaking to you?"

"You noticed."

"Yeah, I noticed. You used to talk about him constantly, and now you don't say a word about him. I figured the honeymoon was over."

"It might be. Would you think I was crazy if I said I wanted to change that?"

Chet waited a long time again to answer. "No," he finally said. "No. But don't ask me for advice because I have no idea."

Galen smiled. "I won't. Mostly, I'm grateful you listened. And that you haven't disowned me."

"Well, that would be effed up. I may not quite get it all, but you're my bro. That doesn't change. Brianna's gonna be blown away, though."

"Unless you don't tell her. I need to talk to Georgie first."

"All right. Mum."

Their food arrived, and it was awkward between them for several more minutes until it wasn't. They eased into other conversation, occasionally coming back to the main topic, and, before long, they laughed and kidded each other.

Chet was a native of Los Angeles, a place where "half my friends are gay" could be true. It might have been true in a million other places, but Galen knew it was true in the City of Angels. Galen wasn't the first queer man Chet knew, and he wouldn't be the last, and by the end of lunch, Chet had comfortably added Galen to his list of queer friends. It had been an okay coming out.

Galen paid the check and dreaded the next person he would tell because he knew it wouldn't be nearly as easy: Georgie.

∞ Chapter 6 ∞

FIGHT AT THE POLICE STATION

GALEN HAD TAKEN THREE DAYS off to clear his mind. The first of the three days was his mother's birthday, and, in line with every year before that, Galen couldn't drag himself out of the house or many places in the house to do much of anything but think and rest and try to keep from thinking more.

As for the extra two days, he told Georgie another lie and claimed the LAPD had pushed him lately and that he wanted a few days away for his mental health. She was a nurse. She understood people who reached their limits. She saw breakdowns and family violence and overdoses and accidents that stress and exhaustion had caused and not only didn't question Galen about his work weariness but congratulated him on knowing himself well enough to take a break.

"I promise to let you have your solitude," she had said. "Especially today." She kissed his cheek. "No pesky calls or requests for favors."

Her sympathy made him feel guilty. The truth was that he took the extra time off to reflect on their life and imagine how it would be if she were no longer in his. But he also thought he did that strange thing for the right reasons. He hoped to be fair to their marriage. He had taken vows and promised to ride out life with Georgie, no matter what they faced. He had to be sure he couldn't stay, even if he desired a life with someone else.

He also wondered if she would be better off without him, even if he never moved on with Michael. She deserved the right life. Whether by a solid marriage or a ticket out, he would try to give her that life and honor his marriage vow to always work toward her happiness.

What complicated it all, and why he needed to be alone for a few days, was the agreement she had wrangled from him to have a baby.

Georgie hadn't known why things had changed between Galen and Michael or why Galen seemed more present than he had been. She couldn't know that the explosion and his kiss with Michael had come between him and Michael. She only knew that things seemed different and had seized the chance to press her strange advantage.

And Galen had, in a moment of weakness and doubt and jealousy over Michael, agreed to start a family with her. He had thought more and more about Georgie giving birth to a child that would be his parents' grandchild. If he couldn't be with Michael, he hoped for a child who would understand the power of his or her legacy and enter the world with the force of its grandparents behind it.

He had begun to want the child, the more she talked about it and the more he thought the chances he would end up with Michael were so minimal as to not count.

Almost instantly he realized that with that decision, he created a minefield, for he wanted and worked for two things that naturally opposed one another—Michael and a child with his wife. He had to watch every step he took very carefully. He had to find a way out.

He wasn't entirely reckless. Georgie had only recently stopped taking the pill, after finishing a cycle to keep her system balanced, and he hoped to find answers before they made a baby.

As he expected, he did nothing to find those answers on the first day, his mother's birthday. He took a shower, put on his favorite sweats and T-shirt, and headed for the couch where he thought about snacks on a school trip and a mother who waved and said, "Have fun," and a smile that said, "I miss you, already," and lasagna and lectures about misbehavior and help with math homework and graduations, from high school and college and the police academy, that she didn't see and Robert, whom he'd always wanted to introduce her to, and a lost ability to tell a real joke and photos of a crime scene, the worst he'd ever seen. Overwhelmed, he fell asleep, to block it out and pass the time, but it was all there again when he woke up. He stared at the ceiling for the rest of the day and thought about all the same things.

The next day, he came back to himself, as he did every other year. His thoughts returned to the present. Alone in the house, he test-drove a breakup with Georgie. He stared at their bed and imagined her in it with someone else. He saw her lithe body moving to the pleasures delivered by another man. A few months earlier, it would have hurt him to see her stepping outside of their bond and allowing another man in to share herself with him, to be so captivated by his desire for her that she thought of nothing and no one else. It would have been covetousness, a wish to have what his rival had, based on a fear of her no longer caring about him more than it would have been possessiveness. It stunned him then, as he stared at their bed, to daydream through her reaching paradise, led there by the prowess of a stranger, and feel very little jealousy. He only wondered by the hour who Michael was with.

He also went online again, from his phone, and conducted a different kind of research. He watched gay porn. He was a man. He could guess at what two men did together, but he couldn't visualize it.

He had been surprised to see how similar some of it was to hetero sex. His favorite videos were by amateurs, who seemed to have real romantic feelings for each other, versus actors in studio porn, although he couldn't be sure what was real and what was contrived. Every scene could have been well-staged theater. Either way, he enjoyed watching men kiss each other and make love in a missionary position. He saw how men touched each other before the main event and noticed how easily they determined roles.

Throughout his Internet travels, he had picked up words such as "frot" and "bear" and "twink" and "raw" and "rim" and "top" and "bottom". He watched a little of it all play out on his phone. He was particularly intrigued by men who frotted while they kissed.

After three days, he was that much farther into gay life, with better answers about his wife and no idea where Michael fit in with him or where he fit in with Michael.

One thing he had determined. He would talk to Georgie about postponing having a baby, even though he had become attached to the idea of carrying on his parents' legacies. He was still unsure whether he would end up with his wife or with Michael or alone, and it seemed unwise to follow through with what he had agreed to in a moment of hurt and distance from Michael. He would have to use condoms for a while until she could ease back into taking the pill. He dreaded that conversation, and he would have it once he was back at work.

Georgie had left him alone, sexually, for the three days he was off, but on the fourth day, the morning he returned to work, she flirted with him. He relied on some quick math he had done regarding her cycle, hoped he had the dates right, and gave in. It further conflicted him, for he had enjoyed it but had mostly thought of Michael through to the climax.

He wondered if, for the rest of their lives, he would make love to her body and Michael's soul, coming to him through images and the love Galen felt, even from the great distance that stood between them.

At work that first day back, he leafed through the updates of events to watch for on patrol.

He spotted a buzz word—"homeless"—and panicked when he read the paragraph surrounding the word.

While he had been out, the city had razed an entire homeless encampment, a large enclave with several tents, and moved out everyone and their belongings—tents, sleeping bags, blankets, carts full of collected items, supplies.

It was a horrifying turn of events.

Galen knew that tent neighborhood. He had been there once, on his first Sunday of outreach. It was an encampment Michael regularly serviced with needed items, he had said. Galen guessed that around thirty people lived there. He remembered that some of them had small dogs that were not only companions but guard dogs.

The displacement of the people and pets in that camp would destroy some of them. Galen already knew as a cop what the challenges were, but he had learned from Michael's stories and seen more as a volunteer in his street clothes, talking to the people Michael helped every day of the week, and he knew the worst of it.

There would be those who simply wouldn't be able to recover from that kind of disruption to their precarious lives. Others would be exposed to crime without neighbors to help keep watch. Still others could be jailed or moved too far away from services to recreate the somewhat stable existence they had in the camp.

Galen was furious with the city. A huge rock formed in his stomach. Michael would be on the warpath. Already, the bicycle police near that encampment had moved out one man, without warning. He had had too many carts, if Galen recalled. Michael had called that bullshit, too, with choice words for the police.

With the latest action, he would wonder why Galen hadn't stopped the raid or at least called to warn him, even though they hadn't spoken in a month, since their kiss, and not meaningfully for a few weeks before that, after the explosion. That wouldn't matter. What happened between them would be immaterial for Michael if the safety of a community he cared about was at stake. He would presume Galen would rise above their personal clashes and do everything he could to help Michael's side, to help people in need, who always came first.

Or don't you protect and serve them, too, cop?

And Galen *would* have protected them, but he hadn't known about the raid. He hadn't been at work.

He reached for his phone to text Michael, and Chet appeared from nowhere and pulled him into the locker room.

Galen held up his phone and said, "Dude, I don't have time, right now. I gotta text Michael."

"No, you don't. He's been around, at different times, looking for you. He seems like a cannon about to fire. I would stay away."

Galen's heart pounded. "He was here?" He pointed at the floor with his phone, to indicate the police station, in general. "Here. He was *here*."

"Yes. Wouldn't say what it was about, but he looked mad."

"Why didn't you call me or text me?"

"I didn't want to butt in! I have *no* idea what's going on, and I don't know if Georgie's in your grill, checking your phone, or what is and isn't a touchy subject right now if I called."

"I hear you. I don't know either, to be honest. I'm sorry. Thanks, man. I still need to text him—"

There was a commotion in the public area of the station. It was loud enough that Galen and Chet heard it from the locker room. They went to investigate.

To Galen's horror, it was Michael. Two officers—Robbens and Markey—each held Michael by an arm. Michael shouted, "I'm not a threat! You grabbed *me*!"

Galen appeared in his line of sight.

"There he is! I just want to talk to that cop right there!"

That cop.

Galen intervened. He had seniority over Robbens and Markey. "It's okay. Let him go. He's not a threat."

Robbens and Markey let Michael go but hovered.

"It's *fine*," Galen said. They grated on Galen's nerves. Michael being in the station made him nervous, and he needed them to disperse so he could have some mental room to deal with his much bigger problem.

"Come on," Chet said, and they left Galen and Michael alone.

"Michael—" Galen said, but that was as far as he got.

"You are the worst!" He didn't lower his voice. "I get that you like to hide, but not giving me a heads up that those good people— *my friends*—homeless people!—were gonna be taken out and then ditching for three days is a fucking joke."

"I—"

"Save it! Because of you, I can't find any of those people! They could be anywhere! Jail, even! This is so effed up!"

"Keep your voice down. For your sake, not mine," Galen said. He dreaded Robbens and Markey returning to lock up Michael if he became too agitated and appeared to be a threat to the station.

"Yeah, you'd like for me to keep quiet." Michael looked right at him, and for a moment, Galen felt that he softened a little, as though seeing Galen took the sting out of a seventy-two-hour rage. It lasted only an instant.

"I came here to tell you that we will sue the shit out of everyone here if anything happens to any of those people you kicked out of the only place they had!"

Galen felt punched. It hurt him that Michael had seemed to think he was capable of not caring that a large group of homeless people's lives were made far worse by the actions of his police department, when the truth was that, had he been there, he would have asked his department to stand down. Barring that, he would have insisted on joining the scene, during the raid, to gather as much information as he could about where people went. He would have slipped people money, if necessary, and even taken anybody truly in a bad way home with him. Georgie was a nurse. She would have understood why he did it. *With no doubt*, he would have called Michael and warned him, even on his mother's birthday. He would have found a way to drag himself out of the house to help.

"Why didn't you text me—"

"Text?!" Michael said. "Text?! So you could hide inside your phone? I wanted answers, *to my face*, about this. So, I showed up here. Every day. And every day, you were somewhere else, anywhere but here, skulking, hiding."

"You know what?" Galen said, "I'm tired of this…*bullshit*, as you like to call it." He raised his voice. "I had nothing to do with that raid. I just found out myself! Don't you think I would have warned you? Who the hell are you to come in here yelling at me like you know what I would have done?!"

A small crowd of coworkers gathered.

Galen heard Chet call his name somewhere in the distance, but he ignored him.

"I don't know anything about you, anymore. Not since you kissed me and didn't know what to do about it."

Galen felt the air around the police station turn mud-thick with the heavy silence that descended on the room. He realized, though, that he wasn't embarrassed about kissing a man. He was simply mortified that everyone knew his business.

All he could do was go with what Michael had unleashed. "I knew exactly what to do. I did it! I kissed you! *You* were the one who walked away!" With those words, he no longer cared, for he was already miserable, and no amount of exposure could make it worse. "*You* were the one who refused to return my texts and calls! *You* hid! *You* didn't know what to do after *I* kissed *you*! *I KISSED YOU!* Not the other way around!" Galen had had those epiphanies during his time away. He had hoped to talk to Michael about them under more private circumstances.

He muddled through the embarrassment of the awkward, non-lovers lovers' quarrel at work, by exposing himself even more, to remove the sting. He called out to the room, "Yes! I kissed a man!" He laughed a fake, exaggerated laugh. "Welcome to L.A.!"

He turned back to Michael, "Leave my job. You threatened to sue. You wanna talk to me, get a lawyer. You've been hiding for a month. Go hide behind your lawyer!" He started to walk away but turned back and added, "Don't ever again accuse me of being too scared of life to live it. Do you know who you're saying that to? Since the day I met you, you've known I don't give rat's *ass* what people think of how I should live. Life is way fucking harder than yelling from the rooftops that I kissed a man. In fact, that's easy! You know why? Because I liked it!" He turned again to the room. "Did everybody catch that? I liked it!"

He walked away. He refused to run for cover in the locker room. He returned to the desk, finished leafing through the day's information, asked for the keys to his patrol car, and left through the door that led to the patrol car parking lot.

In his peripheral vision, he saw Michael leave the station, and something in his heart broke. Something, everything that mattered, unhinged and fell away, went away with Michael.

He thanked Chet, mentally, for not approaching him at the desk to give some kind of, "Hey, sorry that happened, man," speech and making him that much more of a spectacle.

Outside, he started the motor of his patrol car and said aloud to no one, "Who do you think you *are*?"

He was too agitated to patrol and let the car idle. "You come to *my* job, *twice*, yelling at me, all self-righteous. Total. Bullshit."

He heard in his mind over and over the words, *You are the worst!* Those words had wounded him beyond measure.

He turned off the motor and stared out the window.

What's going on, Michael? You confuse me. You worry about me and you yell at me and you kiss me and you run from me.

God, how I love you for coming to see me when you thought I was hurt. God, how it hurts that you think I'm the worst.

Whatever this is, I don't want it to end. I don't want you to be so far away.

He knew then that his life was about to get much worse, for, in the commotion and the pain, the feeling that had most overpowered him, standing there yelling at Michael, with Michael yelling at him, in front of everyone, and caring more about Michael than his own embarrassment or terribly hurt feelings, was need.

There was no doubt in his mind.

He needed Michael.

And he couldn't have him.

∞ Chapter 7 ∞

WeHo

FOR THE FIRST TIME IN a long while, Galen was glad to be home. After his fight with Michael in front of fifteen coworkers and a minor reprimand from his boss, who had said they had all, every officer, seen worse, every single day, from angry arrestees who thought it was all bullshit, than what he and Michael had delivered but that it would be better if, in the future, such conversations didn't come from his officers and that Galen should "take it outside" if he had a problem with a visitor, he looked forward to a quiet dinner with Georgie and turning in early. His fake need for a mental health break had become very real.

The awakening was rude.

There would be no quiet dinner. He wouldn't turn in early. He wouldn't turn in at all, at least not there, ever again. He learned those facts the moment he stepped through the door.

Georgie greeted him with eyes swollen shut from crying. "I have to learn from *Josefina* that you're gay?"

Oh, no.

Josefina was his boss's wife. Galen could guess that all day and into the early evening, while he patrolled, his fellow officers and their significant others had burned up the phone lines to spread the word about THE FIGHT OVER THE KISS BETWEEN GALEN AND A MAN. The only one who hadn't heard, he realized, was Brianna, Chet's girlfriend. She was too new to be in the inner circle. If she had known, Chet would have warned him.

Galen's stupidity in forgetting that the Telephone News would report everything to Georgie was a sign of how distracted he was by his fight with Michael.

Georgie had regained his attention. And he had to face it.

"I don't know that I'm gay. All I know is...."

"You kissed a man and had a huge fight about it all over the police station."

The story carried the usual exaggerations.

"It wasn't all over the police station. It lasted forty-five seconds. I went on patrol. He left."

She shook her head. "None of that matters." She dropped her face into her hands and bawled.

He went to her and hugged her and told her, "Shhh," and kissed her on top of her head, and rested his chin there while she leaned on him, and said, "I'm sorry, Georgie. I'm sorry, Baby Girl," which made her cry harder.

He rocked her gently and kissed her several more times on her warm hair and said, "I'm sorry," between kisses, and, after a while, they talked, about a boy named Noah he had loved in high school and a young man named Robert who slayed his heart in college and stayed on his mind until Galen was twenty-five, when he met Georgie and started to forget, deep attachments that were uncommon for friendship but natural for romantic love.

He confessed all. His complex attraction to her, the way he felt about men, the kiss with Michael under the streetlight.

Michael had been the hardest to explain. He was her direct rival and the person Galen loved more. But Galen loved Georgie in a different way, and it pained him deeply to see her hurt. She hadn't driven him away with bitchiness or cheating or incompatibility of temperament. She was a good person, and he was crazy about her in a very particular way. He wished he loved her the way he should have, the way she deserved to be loved, especially considering the wonderful way she loved him. She gave everything, all of herself, in trust and because she had faith in him and in their marriage. She wanted him, of everyone in the world, to be the father of her child, to be the one person to whom she would be forever connected because they shared children.

With it upon him, for real and not as a fake run-through, as it had been literally just earlier that day, before he left for work, he was scared to say goodbye to his friend Georgie, who had been with him for eight years, five of them as his wife, who had let him enjoy the riches of having such a beautiful person for a wife, who had given him a family and someone with whom to be in an unconditional partnership. She teased him about his bad barbecuing and watched every crime show ever made with him and let him see her naked and touch her body. She gave herself to him freely, entirely, every time, with no reservations. Almost a decade of history and intimacy and private jokes and attachment was hard to lose.

And, yet, he lost it, all of it, right there in his living room, while he hugged her tight and tried to explain the queer side of himself, which he hoped to make her understand was all of who he was and not merely a side. His queerness *was*, the way *he* was, and that was all.

He had practiced for two days for the moment into which Josefina—and he and Michael and their argument and their kiss and their budlike relationship that had poked through the earth and blossomed into something he hoped hadn't died—had catapulted him. Faced with how hurt Georgie was, he was ill-prepared. It hurt far worse than he had expected. He fumbled through it.

After several hours of tears and consternation and the slamming of things, he packed a few necessities and went to Chet's. He would stay just long enough to find a small apartment, he had said. Chet was okay, either way. He was at Brianna's half the time anyway, *he* had said.

Eight days later, Galen moved into a split-level studio apartment in West Hollywood. The living area, closet, bathroom, and tiny kitchen were downstairs, in the same square space.

Upstairs, a little loft just large enough for bedroom furniture and a little privacy hovered over the downstairs. It kept Galen from having to kick his guests off a couch, just so he could pull it out to make a bed. The West Hollywood location had less to do with Michael and more to do with wanting to live in a neighborhood with a thriving gay community.

He cried more than he thought he would, nights and days by himself, about change and all that was no longer part of his life.

He missed Georgie, who filed for divorce. Michael had said he was the worst, and he felt like it vis-à-vis Georgie. As a cop, he had broken up many fights between couples who had split up, who made life miserable for each other out of resentment, and he swore he would make the entire process easy on Georgie.

He spoke only kind words about her at work. His contrite, despairing mood, which was honest, would be reported back to Georgie. It wouldn't save their marriage or his face, but it would give her as much dignity as possible, under the circumstances.

She never did, but she could have called him a miscreant and disparaged him around the station, and he would have said, "She's right." He wouldn't engage. He had stolen too much from her. He owed her every win, forever, not for being gay, but because he let himself fall in love with someone who wasn't her, the person he had married and who had a right to expect love and devotion from her husband, and because of the broken promises.

She had called a few days after he left and asked him a question. She cried through it.

He shed tears, too.

"Never mind that I found out in the worst way."

The worst.

"Can you just tell me?" she said. "What did I miss? Was this always there? Why did you marry me if your heart wasn't in it?"

"It's always been there, but we missed it because of how captivated I was—and am—by you." It had been the truth. "You're sexy and I love you and we missed it. I married you because I love you, but we missed that I'm wired to love men more, the right way, the romantic way. I haven't figured out the sex part yet, but this is right, Georgie. You deserve better than what I am for you."

"Did I ever make you happy?"

"Oh, yes, Baby G—"

"Don't. Say it." Her voice was tight and strained.

"All right. I won't." Slow tears rolled down his face. "I won't say it. But you did. You made me happy constantly. And maybe more importantly, you made me want to make you happy. I love you. And I admire you, Georgie."

And she cried some more, soft tears, not hard, bawling ones, and said, "I love you, too," and hung up.

He spent two more weeks in constant shock, shock that Georgie was no longer there, shock that he lived away from his wife and his life, shock that he began to think of himself as gay.

He slowly came out of the fog and returned to functioning, for survival's sake. He went through familiar motions, grateful for the ease of a well-memorized routine, and embraced what lay ahead.

In the divorce, he proceeded without an attorney and told Georgie's lawyer Georgie could have whatever she wanted. As it turned out, she only wanted her share.

He was persona non-grata at work for about ten days until the job heated up in the field and he proved to be the excellent back-up he always was, and his fellow officers said, "Let Galen and Georgie work it out. I'm staying out of it."

A few of them were squeamish about his being gay, but it was Los Angeles, and he wasn't the only gay officer. In the eighties, another officer had sued and paved the way for gay officers to serve without harassment. Lessons had been learned. There was some gay-shaming locker-room banter that disgusted Galen, but it didn't mean Galen couldn't be gay and a cop.

Chet had been a true best friend. He treated Galen like nothing had happened. He joked with him in the open and helped normalize his existence. That was the final nail in the coffin of persecution. People moved on to other things, and THE SAGA OF GALEN AND GEORGIE moved off-stage. Even Galen's sexuality became a non-subject, at least to his face.

With Georgie's permission, he slipped into their house while she was at the hospital and picked up a few more things and moved them into his apartment. He only had room for the bare minimum in his tiny new space, but it had helped to have some meaningful possessions in his new world.

On his days off, he explored the neighborhood. He envied gay men walking down the street holding hands or letting their arms touch as they strolled, men who knew who they were and who had gotten a major head start on where Galen was and had used their lives more wisely and found somebody to share themselves with long before Galen figured out who he was.

And, finally, he geared up to face down what—and whom— he knew he had to confront.

Michael.

∞ Chapter 8 ∞

KNOCK AND ANNOUNCE

GALEN KNOCKED SOFTLY. HE HAD no idea what went on behind the door—wild sex, cheese-puff gluttony, reading. He only knew he was unexpected, and there was a good chance the door would be slammed in his face.

What he got was a close second. Michael opened his apartment door and leveled a cold stare at Galen.

For a moment, Galen simply stood there and took in Michael, his face, his countenance, his being. It was all there. The calm demeanor, the witty aura, the compassionate vibe. Galen also admired the tan skin, the cleft chin, and the neat eyebrows. As much as he missed Georgie, he hadn't longed for her, not really, anyway. He longed for moments and essences and beats, memories, even habits, routines, but he hadn't longed to be near her. He longed for Michael, with everything in him. He missed their talks and their unexpected intimacy and their brotherhood.

At last, he said, "May I come in?"

"No." Michael moved to close the door, but Galen gently pushed it back with one hand.

"Get outta here, cop. And lose the door code. You proved where your loyalties lie when you and your city were too miserly to share some sidewalk, and my friends got evicted from the little bit of space they had found for themselves."

Galen had expected that. He answered calmly. "I told you. I was away from the station when that happened."

"Yeah, and you had no idea it was coming."

"That's right. I had no idea it was coming. If I had, I would have warned you. I would have tried to stop it. I would have been there to help the people getting kicked out if I couldn't stop it."

"Well, it's over, anyway."

"Maybe technically, but not actually."

"What does that mean? Are more raids planned? What in the hell—"

"No, no. At least, not that I know of." He looked hard at Michael to show that he was telling the truth. "I mean it. Nothing that I know of is planned. I was talking about you. You intend to punish me permanently for something I couldn't help."

"Hm. Well, I can't forgive what I can't forgive."

Galen nodded. "Hm," he said, too. "I didn't realize you had a crystal ball. Must be convenient. Must make things much easier."

"Okay, I'll bite. What is that supposed to mean?"

"It means you're able to tell who's in pain and who's not, who needs help and who doesn't, even if the ball is calibrated, or whatever they do to crystal balls, wrong."

"What are you talking about?"

"I'm talking about how sure you are that I was away from the station for reasons within my control, to skulk and hide from you. That I wasn't down, for the count, in terrible pain somewhere, maybe shot, maybe shocked. Just your friends in the homeless camp were in a world of hurt. No one else." He turned to leave.

"Hold on. Are you okay? Did something happen?"

"Ahh, now he asks. I've been trying to give you the answer to that question for a long time. Well, I'm a cop and you're a private citizen. Your wish that I vacate the premises is my command." He headed for the brass elevator.

When he got downstairs and reached the sidewalk, his phone pinged. He checked it.

What do you mean, 'shot'?

Galen stared at his phone.

I wasn't shot, he finally texted.

I'm relieved.

Your crystal ball is still way out of whack. Have a good one.

∞

Galen found a way to drive to work that avoided Michael's apartment. He never headed in that direction unless there was no other way to get somewhere.

Large grocery stores, however, were in short supply in the denser parts of Los Angeles. Galen used the same store he guessed Michael used.

That guess proved correct the day Galen picked through oranges in the produce department, hoping to find the perfect ones in the slight off-season, and looked up to see Michael sizing up the Gala apples.

Galen almost let his oranges go so he could back away from his cart and leave the store, but it was his grocery store, too. He lived in the neighborhood, and he was as entitled to buy his produce at that store as Michael was.

He didn't go back to selecting oranges, though. He also refused to stare longingly.

"Hi, Michael," he called out gently.

Michael looked up, startled. He seemed to have recognized the voice before he saw the face and was shocked by the confirmation his eyes provided him. He tentatively approached the oranges, and Galen.

"What brings you to this store?"

"Technically, the fact that it's a store and it's open for business is all the reason I need to be here. Nothing needs to bring me here." After another moment, he said, "I live near here."

Michael looked baffled.

"No, I am not stalking you. I stay as far away from your apartment as possible, which isn't easy, logistically, considering where I live. This just happens to be the only good grocery store around here." He went back to selecting oranges.

Michael stared at him.

He found five good oranges and moved to the Roma tomatoes.

Michael followed him. "What do you mean, you live near here?"

"Well, that's another question you're asking too late." He picked six tomatoes and headed to the red onions.

Michael followed again. "Where's Georgie?"

"To quote you, that's none of your goddamned business."

Michael's jaw fell open.

Galen chose two onions, maneuvered his cart out of another shopper's way, and wheeled on to the dairy section.

∞

I noticed at the store today that you weren't wearing your wedding ring, but you never do, so I don't know what to think, the text read.

Galen stared at the words for a long time.

He never answered.

∞

A few days later, Michael texted, *I know it's short notice, but if you really are in the area, I'd like to see you. I don't want to invite myself over, but would you like to drop by here? I know what I said, but the code is still 2-3-4-5.*

Galen meant what he texted back. *I don't feel like figuring out whether I'm going to run into Paul. I worked past that fear when I knocked on your door the last time. Can't do it again. This is me, "the worst", staying away, like I should, as the evil cop that I am.*

∞

Michael texted a few nights later, *I've talked around this like a coward long enough. I'm sorry I wouldn't hear you out. I'm sorry for calling you "the worst" and treating you like you were nothing but an unfeeling cop. Can we please get together on Sunday at my place to talk? That is, if you don't have plans with Georgie? I will skip rounds and let someone else in the office pick it up, for once. Let me know. Hope to see you.*

Galen never looked away from the phone while he determined what to do. He stared so hard at the phone, his gaze turned into a dreamy fog and the phone became a blurry image as he wondered how to reply. Finally, he texted, *Sure. I'll be there at noon.*

Great. Looking forward to it.

Galen could only withhold for a short while before he texted, *Me, too.*

I miss you.

Me, too, you.

∞

"Thanks for coming." Michael opened the door wide.

Galen stepped into the apartment he knew well. It was a homecoming mixed with trepidation. He looked with fondness at the *Ben-Hur* poster on his way through the hallway to the living room.

Once there, Michael said, "Please, sit down. Wherever you like."

Galen headed for his favorite huge leather chair. They both smiled a little at the familiar move.

They sat, and neither of them spoke.

"This is ridiculous," Michael finally said.

"Don't you mean bullshit?"

"That, too. What are we doing? What is going on? Let me finally ask you. What happened?"

With those two words, Galen felt the pain dissipate. He had been stressed and filled with the dread of hurting Georgie and burdened by the weight of self-discovery while feeling the freedom self-discovery gave him after he had been penned in by so much history and sadness and overwhelmed with the grief of losing Michael. He felt displaced in his own existence and wasn't sure if he mourned his old life or longed for what he sensed could only come from his uncertain future with a fear that he wouldn't get it. With Michael's simple question, some of his immediate burdens fell away.

He spoke plainly and without defense. "I came out to Chet, and from there—"

"Wait. Came out-came out? Like, *came out*?"

"It's complicated, but it's also very clear that I'm queer, or something like it. Maybe homosexual, maybe heterosexual—that's the complex part—for sure homoromantic. Like I said, it's complicated."

He shared everything that had happened, from the moment he came out to Chet, to his time away from the station, except the part about his mother's birthday, to Georgie finding out about their argument in front of everyone over their kiss, to his impending divorce and move to West Hollywood. He revealed that it was his attraction to Georgie's androgyny that made him wonder whether he was even heterosexual. He withheld the most important elements of his new life: He loved Michael and needed him, very much.

"I don't expect you to welcome me with open arms, but I would at least like to talk about why we're suddenly in enemy camps. I…kissed you, and you kissed me back, for real, and not just to prove a point. I felt it. And then you walked away and shut me out and blamed me for the separation. I was away during the raid partly because I was trying to understand that."

"I did blame you for the distance between us."

"Do you still?"

"I do." There was no anger in him. He sounded sad.

"Why?"

"Because you were experimenting with me, and *on* me, that night. You had no intention of leaving your wife. You *were* proving a point, even if I also felt you kissed me for real. It's why I dared you to do it, but I wasn't in the mood for that. 'Gay-curious'. Been there, suffered that."

Galen had read about that on several blogs over the previous weeks, especially the ones about attraction, which was where he had spent the bulk of his time.

He had no answer for Michael. It had been true. He had kissed Michael under the streetlight on a dare to himself. Michael had said, "Do it," but Galen had really dared *himself* to kiss Michael and dared Michael to respond, on his way to a date with another man. It had been insensitive to play with Michael's emotions that way and treat him as though he were an object.

"And you treated my life like it was a game or a bit of theater, there for your ridicule and enjoyment, asking me if I was 'fucking'," he made air quotes, "Paul, like all I was capable of was 'screwing'," he made more air quotes, "because, what, I'm gay? Because two men together don't rise to the level of you and your wife? Because we're not entitled to dignity and privacy? Because we couldn't have fallen in love and wanted to be together? Because you weren't willing to ask yourself who you are, so everything and everyone else became a joke? Nothing was serious? Kiss the gay guy before his date?"

Galen's heart pounded with shame about his behavior and with fear that Michael had fallen in love with Paul.

"The ultimate erasure of gay existence is to determine from the outside that you will set the norms and the boundaries and decide the tone of the interactions, as though you have authority over all of it because you come from what you see as a place of legitimacy, of normalcy, like gayness is a deviant to be wrangled and handled as you see fit."

Galen was so embarrassed, he suddenly wished he hadn't come there. He felt ignorant and foolish for expecting Michael to return his texts and phone calls after the way he had treated him. He was deeply ashamed, and not because he thought he might be gay and could sympathize. He had behaved deplorably.

"I am...very, very ashamed and embarrassed and surprised and grateful you asked me to come here."

"Well, I was right until I was wrong. I did the exact same thing to you. I treated you like your life as a straight cop made it impossible to hurt you and like you already had a weird advantage, so all bets and decency were off."

"You're right about it all, and more on the side of right than wrong when it comes to who maybe messed up more. I came here prepared to fight it out again, but you're right. I'm very, very sorry. All I can say is that, no matter how callous I was, it would never spill over into letting your friends lose their homes without speaking up. None of them—none of any of it—has been a joke to me, despite how I acted."

I was jealous. If only you knew how much I hated the thought of you with another man. I can't tell you now. It's pathetic, and I handled it wrong, anyway.

Michael met Galen's eyes with his own. Galen didn't avoid his stare and let Michael scrutinize him.

"Apology accepted," Michael said. "And, for what it's worth, I believe you that you had no idea about the raid. Pretty narcissistic of me to think you were so caught up about us, you would let other people suffer so horribly. I'm sorry I didn't ask what happened."

"Apology accepted here, too. More than anything else, I'm glad you believe me." He smiled to cover his pain. He loved Michael, more than he did when he knocked on the door. He sensed that they would never really work it out and be together. They may have called a truce, but he couldn't see a way forward. Too much had happened, it seemed. His journey toward himself and happiness in a life that made sense would be a long one.

After a few awkward seconds ticked by, Galen stood up and said, "Well, then. I guess I should go."

"Oh." Michael stood too and seemed surprised. "You're leaving already?"

"I think I should." His smile lost some of its faux mirth.

"Listen, I—"

"No, it's okay. I really should go. You said it yourself. I need to understand that a lot may have occurred in your life, while I was in it and while I was away. I don't want to tread on you...or anyone else."

"Okay." Michael sounded regretful, but Galen saw no reason for it. Michael had spoken the truth.

They started for the door. "So, WeHo," Michael said. He smiled good-naturedly, trying to smooth Galen's exit, Galen figured, but he seemed uneasy.

"WeHo," Galen said. "But like I said, I'm not stalking you. I just like the neighborhood. I always have, well, since we've known each other. It'll be a nice place to find myself. And, the apartment was small enough and cheap enough to suit my need to let Georgie keep everything else."

"I see," he nodded. "You may not believe me, but I'm sorry about Georgie."

"I believe you. And, you know I don't like to use my parents, but now that we've tried to clear up what happened, I just wanted to let you know that one of the days I was away from the station, during the raid, was my mother's birthday. I was very checked out from everything. Well, except my own head."

Michael put his hand to his mouth. "I'm sorry."

Galen gently tugged at Michael's arm and lowered his hand. "No. No. I didn't tell you for that reason. I don't want sympathy. I'm the guilty party, and I guess I'm just hoping to really prove that I was away and distracted. That's all."

"And that my crystal ball is out of whack." He sighed. "I feel like an idiot."

"Don't. Don't. There was no way for you to know. It's me who feels bad. I appreciate your telling me what bothered you. I'm trying to learn more every day. I needed your frankness. And today is certainly a different day from that one. As I said, the actual day is the only real rough one." He smiled a little. "I'm good."

"Okay." Michael nodded in a friendly way and smiled, too.

They reached the door.

"Is your car parked far?"

"I walked. I'm just a few long blocks away. You know how L.A. is. A fabulous place like this," he looked around the foyer, "and down the street, tucked away, you run into a building no one cares about. I'm in one of those."

He smiled to keep things light, so he could leave on decent terms. If that was all he would have, he would take it and be thankful.

Michael returned the smile, but he seemed wistful. "As long as it works for you." He opened the door.

"It does. For now."

"Oh." Michael frowned. "So, you might be moving on?"

Galen sighed. "Well, the weird thing is, the money in my trust...from my parents' house...it's considered separate property from what I had with Georgie." He shrugged. "Who knew? I would have happily given her whatever she wanted, but that's not who she is. So, I might finally dip into it...and maybe buy a place somewhere."

"Oh."

"You never know. Anyway, take it easy."

"You, too."

∞

That night, Galen's phone chimed.

It's not fair. You know where I live, but I don't know where you live.

Galen grinned. He texted Michael his address.

Chapter 9

HARD LESSONS

IT HAD BEEN FOUR MONTHS since Galen and Michael had kissed under the streetlight. Almost three months had passed since Galen had moved away from Georgie and made his way to WeHo. That had been in October.

It was the beginning of January and colder than usual for Los Angeles. Despite the impending long winter, Galen had hope. He and Michael had seen each other at the grocery store and worked things out in late October. In the beginning of that awkward phase when they became neighbors from a distance, Galen kept his promise not to go near Michael's apartment without an invitation. And Michael had treated Galen like a person and not an enemy cop.

Slowly, they had spent more time together. First, on Sundays, then, as the weeks passed, on weeknights. They had started easy.

They e-mailed and texted. They went to dinner. They watched movies in each other's apartments and cut evenings short, each too shy or respectful or scared to do anything more, Galen figured, although he couldn't say for sure how Michael felt because they never broached the subject. Galen knew, at least, that he was too afraid to talk about the dynamics of their seeing each other. He had settled for being grateful for what access he had.

Thanksgiving week had arrived, and Galen wondered about Georgie and missed the routine of going to her sister's house for a large gathering. He had accepted, though, that he would spend Thanksgiving alone.

He was surprised, then, when one day during the middle of a long shift patrolling in the rain, Michael called to invite him to his house for a "party for the holiday" he had called it.

Galen had accepted with joy. He was not only relieved not to spend the day alone, but he was excited to see Michael and hoped to reconnect with some of Michael's friends, the ones who were in Galen's phone, even though they had rarely contacted each other since the first party, when he had met them. He prayed Paul wasn't invited.

A present awaited him when the day arrived. He stepped into Michael's apartment to find the table set for two. Clouds dimmed the natural light that came through the large living room window, but the sun received help from a fire that blazed in Michael's fireplace. The house smelled of many delicious foods.

"Isn't anybody else coming?"

Michael looked tousled and handsome toggling between kitchen and hosting duties.

"No. Just us," he said. He smiled and stared for a moment at Galen. "Is that okay?"

"Yes," Galen said. He smiled, too. "It's okay."

And Galen had helped in the kitchen, and they never ran out of things to talk about, not while they stuffed mushrooms or ate seven courses or lounged in the living room and fought off the sleep brought on by turkey tryptophan.

It had gone well, and it had led to other days, mostly Sundays, and more weeknights and the occasional spontaneous day off, too.

And Galen had introduced Michael to his favorite thing.

"The beach? In December?" Michael had said.

"This is the best time for the beach," Galen had said. "Water's actually at its warmest, after the long summer of sunshine heating it up. And people don't know it. As big as this city is, there are days and days when no one is on the beach, right now. It's like paradise. You have it all to yourself."

And they had spent the day walking along it in their long sweats and hoodies, with bare feet. And on another day, they had done it again, and then again.

And Michael had taken to the solitude a day on the beach in winter had given him and Galen. It had become "their" thing.

As Christmas approached, Galen made no assumptions. He had no plans, but he figured Michael would want to see other friends since he had spent Thanksgiving with Galen. He had bought Michael a present that he expected to give him sometime after Christmas.

He was stunned again when, on Christmas Eve, Michael had phoned and asked if he could stop by in the early evening. Galen had happily accepted the reverse invitation. He thought they might spend twenty minutes politely exchanging gifts, but Michael had arrived with a full meal in tow and turned Galen's small apartment into a cozy lair. He stayed well past midnight. He said he wanted to be the first to wish Galen a merry Christmas.

Soon, much of their free time was spent together. Whether they handed out items in the streets to get people through the cold days and nights or caught a movie or hunkered down in each other's living rooms or enjoyed a meal one of them had cooked, Galen was just happy to be on such good terms with Michael.

And he watched his own perspective broaden the more he traveled in Michael's orbit. No matter what happened between them, Michael had made him a far better police officer than he was the night they met.

I need you, he thought so much of the time they were together. *And I want to be someone you need.*

As January arrived, they began to check with each other before making plans elsewhere. They coordinated their errands and ran them together. Sometimes, they ran each other's errands or grabbed something extra for each other at the grocery store.

In all their time together, they had been chaste. They hadn't even kissed. Galen had been unwilling to take liberties a second time, after the kiss under the streetlight had offended Michael, and he wasn't sure he would know what to do if things escalated beyond another kiss. He shied away from it all. And Michael made no advances on Galen, possibly fearful Galen was "gay-curious" and not gay or possibly because Michael wasn't interested in more than a deep friendship.

Galen was unsure what to call what they were, and he was terrified Michael would become tired of the limbo—if he felt they *were* more than friends—and the lack of a physical relationship between them and turn elsewhere.

He wasn't sure Michael didn't have liaisons with other men, Paul, or someone else. He blocked out the idea and relegated it to something to the side of what he and Michael had, but it scared him. And he had learned his lesson about belittling Michael's life. He understood that Michael's other pursuits may have been dead serious and more important to Michael than his connection to Galen. He harbored simmering jealousies.

Then one day, Galen thought his fears had come true. He and Michael were at the beach. It was barely fifty degrees outside, but the sun shone bright, even as the waves sounded ominous.

"How long are we gonna do this?" Michael said.

Gulls cawed and filled the silence Galen left between them, as he pondered the question with dread. He wondered if it was over between them before it had fully flourished.

He didn't bother with a perfunctory, "What do you mean?" Instead he said, "I don't know. I know I can't ask you to do this forever, and if you're about to tell me you can't do it anymore, I understand."

"You do?" He looked upset.

"Well, I mean, after the streetlight, the kiss, I know to tread lightly, and I can't expect you to live like this—"

"Like what?" He stopped walking. Galen did too. They faced each other. Their feet were two inches deep in the cool water.

Michael was annoyed.

Galen was nervous. He answered the question. "In a sexless...relationship, or whatever this is—"

"I can't believe you could just let me go that easily." It was clear his feelings were very hurt. "You're *always* such a logical cop."

"Who said it would be easy? I would hate it. I would absolutely hate it. I've been there, without you. It's horrible." He was resolute. "It just...makes sense. And...maybe you have feelings for someone else—"

"*What?*"

"I respect your life, Michael. That's all I meant."

"Sometimes, your police officer approach is really...hard to deal with. Just the facts, and that's it. You've analyzed it all and are sure you're right because the facts make you think you are."

"Yes. Earlier lessons learned. No presumptions made about us, about you."

"No, you're making lots of assumptions about me. Feelings for someone else? When I spend every spare minute with you."

Galen really had learned his lesson about impulsive comments. He was afraid to interject and share how he felt about Paul, about how jealous he was of the things he couldn't see that left unanswered questions between him and Michael. His default was silent deference.

"I appreciate your respect. I do. I get it, and I like it, but did it ever occur to you that you could still have your facts wrong and that I don't want to go anywhere?"

"I wasn't sure—"

"That you're the only person I want to be with for the rest of my life?"

"If—"

"Because I love you?"

"You what?"

Waves crashed in the distance and brought new water to their feet. The cold sand and tiny pebbles that ran between Galen's toes felt strange to him as he processed what he had heard.

What did Michael just say?

Michael stepped in and kissed Galen. "I love you," he said when the kiss ended. "I love you."

And they kissed again, with their feet in the ocean and the sound of the birds in flight along the shore singing approval.

It felt incredible, in the real sense of the word—hard to believe. Galen had craved that feeling since the first time he enjoyed it under the streetlight, and it revisited him and proved more exquisite on the second pass.

They broke away and talked, shared words they had held in for months.

"I've been in love with you since you offered me your phone outside the police station that first night."

"You're in love with me?" The question was a shy one, full of real surprise.

"Yes." Michael kissed him. Galen drank it in and became dizzy.

"For that long? This whole time?"

"Yes."

They kissed again.

"That means while we were driving to WeHo that first night—"

"I already loved you. I don't know that I knew it then, but I understood it later. There was something about that moment outside

the station, about you and the contradiction of you standing there as
a policeman, offering me your phone in real sympathy, and getting
your feelings hurt when I turned it down—I saw it on your face—
that opened a door. And then hearing why you joined the force,
because of your parents. And listening to you talk about the pain you
went through trying to recover from that. I don't know. I've loved
you ever since. And I think about…the craziest things."

"Like what. Tell me."

"I think all the time about…finally having a family, the one I
talked about that night. With you. I see you and me and kids in our
film noir apartment. I daydream about it constantly." He kissed
Galen deeply. "Does that sound strange? A family? With me?"

Galen kissed Michael with tenderness. "No, it doesn't sound
strange."

"You don't think I sound silly?"

"No, I think I *feel* silly, for making all the wrong
assumptions."

They kissed.

"For years, I had been running," Michael said, "but this
happened so suddenly, I didn't know how to run away from it in
time, and then I stopped wanting to run, but you chased me away,
with Georgie and questions about Paul and telling me to go away
after you got hurt in that explosion. I didn't think we'd ever be
together, for real. I've been miserable and euphoric about you."

"I'm sorry for pushing you away." He kissed Michael, in
apology, but the kiss had sexual overtones. The sexiness of kissing
Michael thrilled Galen. The cold ocean air blew around them but not
between them. They held each other close and enjoyed the privacy of
being the only ones on the beach and breathed in the salty air that
reminded them they were alive and basked in the splendor of the
breadth of the wide-open universe around them, demonstrated by

the unending sea. To Galen, anything and everything seemed possible at that moment.

When they stopped kissing, Michael said, "The whole time you were away from me, I loved you more. And over these past months, that love has grown. Is it strange to love someone so soon after meeting them?"

"Well, if it is, then I'm strange because I love you, too, and it took me a while to realize it, too, but I've loved you since the jail cell—"

Michael cut him off. He broke away and did a little dance in the water and splashed and laughed out loud. His face showed pure joy.

"You love me, too?" He laughed again with glee. "You love me?"

"Yes," Galen said. He laughed too and took Michael's hands in his and danced a little too. "Yes!" he shouted. "I love you!"

And they danced around in the water together, enjoying the waves pounding the shore with a distinct bass tone that thinned to a treble song of shallow water drifting in around their feet.

"You love me!"

"I love you!"

And they danced some more.

"I was so unsure. I didn't know what you wanted. I just knew how I felt," Michael said.

Galen pulled him close.

"I want *you*. I love *you*. It's why I was already ruining my marriage, long before the real split, fighting to be with you, and why I was so jealous of Paul and why I screwed up and acted like an ape. I've been miserable and euphoric, too."

"To quote you, that means that when we drove to WeHo—"

"I already loved you. It's why I talked to you about my parents. I know that, now."

They exchanged several kisses, some long, some short. It went on so long, the tide had risen a little and reached their mid-chins, in the place where they had stopped dancing, and still they embraced and kissed.

"We should move, you know."

"I know."

And they moved a little away from the tide and resumed kissing.

Amid their bliss, it was the logical Galen who pulled away and broached the one subject that still lay between them.

"I'm just terrified because I don't know if I can…be with you."

"I know you are." They kissed again. "But we love each other. That is the grandest thing we could have on our side."

"It is. I know. I know."

"I'll be there for you. Don't you feel safe with me?"

"Very. But I don't want to disappoint you. My sexuality is foreign to me."

"But it's not weird or different." They exchanged small pecks. "It's actually quite common." He smiled. "We can get through it, together. I love you, Galen. Let me be with you. I want that, so badly. I've wanted it for a long time. I just wasn't sure how you felt. I have been afraid to say anything, until today. I love you so much, and here on this beach, our place, I couldn't hold it in anymore." They kissed. "Let me show you how much I love you and want to be with you."

The power of the breeze and the sounds of the sea encouraged Galen. They swelled together as a metaphor for two forces that belonged with one another and pushed him along.

But fear also ran through him. He worried about not being good enough, about everything stopping before it started because of his ineptness at lovemaking or his lack of response, about looking foolish and turning off Michael, about never getting a second chance to get it right if he got it wrong the first time. He shared those thoughts, there on the beach, knowing only the birds overheard him.

"Don't be afraid," Michael whispered. "Trust that I would never leave because it's hard for you. I've got you. I love you, and I've got you. I'm not here to judge you. I just want to be with you. You can have as much time as you need. Let me take you home, to your place, where you're comfortable, and prove it to you."

"All right."

All the way home, they talked as they usually did, except that Michael occasionally reached out from the driver's side and stroked Galen's arm or his thigh or his cheek, to reassure him that he need not fear what would happen when they arrived at Galen's.

At Galen's apartment, Michael gave Galen no time for second thoughts. He took Galen's hand and led him upstairs, to Galen's bedroom in the loft.

"I want to finally see you," Michael said.

Galen knew what he meant, but he couldn't move.

Michael took off his own clothes. "Now, you have no reason to be shy. Your turn."

Galen undressed and stood before Michael, who immediately grew in response to seeing Galen naked.

Michael's overt sexual reaction buoyed Galen's confidence. He experienced his own thrill at the intimacy of seeing Michael naked. He liked Michael's body, the firm tones, the masculine, slender waist, the soft skin at his sides that he longed to touch. He couldn't believe his nude body stood so close to another man wearing no clothes. He thought it a miracle after wanting Michael for so long that he waited, naked in Galen's bedroom, for Galen to make love with him. All barriers between them had been stripped away.

And something new happened, something electrifying, something hopeful. His own body reacted, ever so slightly. He knew what it was, and for the first time since he had locked Michael in a jail cell and become prisoner of his heart, his mind and body linked and responded to Michael in unity and in unison.

He and Michael kissed, and Galen took in the warmth of Michael's body against his own. On instinct, his wrapped his arms around Michael's waist. That first touch felt like their first kiss had, and Galen luxuriated in it and pulled Michael closer.

He felt Michael's hard organ touching him, and he fed a deep need to kiss Michael harder with long, unabashed kisses. It still exhilarated him and made him giddy to feel his own lips on those of another man and to enjoy the texture and the pressure and the surprising softness.

Michael guided him to the bed and pulled him down onto it. They lay together and kissed and touched each other's backs and legs and bottoms. The permission to do so excited Galen.

Nothing stands between us, not the police station or my doubts or your disappointment. They're gone, and I'm touching you wherever I want for as long as I want.

When Galen's hands stroked Michael's bottom, the familiar enjoyment of touching a firm behind came to Galen, only Michael's felt grander to Galen than any other time he had cradled someone's rear end in his hands.

His body responded, and he gloried in the reaction, for he thought he might be able to give Michael what he wanted.

They fell into a wonderful rhythm of kissing and stroking each other wherever their hands would reach, except for the one place, below, that Michael hinted at on Galen's body with purposeful near misses with his hands and that, on Michael's body, Galen was still scared to explore, even as he felt the organ against his waist.

"It's okay. Touch me if you want to," Michael said between kisses.

"I've never…stroked another man. Will you…you know. Will I…?"

They never stopped kissing and rocking.

"No, you won't send me over the edge," Michael said. He smiled. "You'll lead me to it, though."

They both chuckled and kissed more.

Galen summoned a final bit of courage and brought his hand to Michael's midriff and let it explore everything there. His hand enclosed around the one place he had never envisioned he'd enjoy the ecstasy of touching and moved up and down. Michael rocked harder, and Galen's own body reacted. He thought he might take himself over the edge from the sensation of Michael in his hand.

A moment later, Michael stroked him and pushed him closer to the top. He kept his mouth on Galen's and said, "Keep your eyes closed. Let yourself feel it, my hand touching you like no one's ever touched you there before."

He hit the right spots, and Galen became stone hard and long in Michael's hand. "Oh, God," Galen said.

Their mouths never stopped touching as Michael gently moved Galen's hand from his own body and used his own enlarged organ to take care of Galen's. He made sure the two of them touched always. He eased into a rhythm that let them slide against each other.

We're frotting, Galen thought.

With his two free hands Michael caressed Galen's behind and continued giving attention from the front, with a slow, steady, rhythmic movement of his hips.

Galen barely maintained control.

Michael gently rolled Galen onto his back and lay on top of him.

"I don't know if I can."

"You don't have to know. We're already making love. This is what it means to make love to a man. Go with it, Babe. Go with me, Galen. *Come* with me."

They rocked back and forth. Michael had lined up their fronts, so that they rubbed each other just right as they moved in a perfect groove.

"You feel so good. That feels so good," Galen said. He held onto his control, barely.

"And how does this feel?" Michael said, and he moved his mouth to Galen's hard maleness.

Galen groaned and arched his back. "Oh. My. God."

"Settle in. I'm gonna blow you like you've never been blown before. I know what feels good, and I'm gonna make you feel good."

Galen could not believe another man's mouth was all over him and felt better than anything he had experienced in his entire life.

Forever, it seemed, Michael toyed with Galen, brought him to the edge and walked him back. When he knew Galen couldn't stand it anymore, he brought him to the end, and drank it all in. Galen shouted and groaned and gyrated, in exultation.

When it was done, Michael rested on top of him and kissed him.

"That was incredible." Galen leaned up and kissed Michael hard and tasted some of himself in Michael's mouth. "You are incredible. I've never…."

"I know, and I intend to make sure it's not the last time you feel that way."

"I didn't know that was possible."

"It is. That, and a whole lot more." Michael became serious. He hugged Galen from above and brought him close. "But don't worry. I don't want you to feel any pressure. I get where you are with this, with us."

They kissed for a long while, with Michael relaxed on top of Galen. Galen felt loved and nurtured and protected.

He gathered his courage, with Michael so close to him and making him feel so safe.

"I feel such a connection with you. I didn't know I could feel this way about anyone or with anyone. I really love you, Michael. I'm very, very happy."

"I love you, too. And, I know you're worried, but I'm very happy, too."

"I am worried."

"Don't be. We'll get there."

Galen surprised himself. "Maybe sooner than you think. I'm feeling like I want to kiss you, *there*. I just don't think I know what I'm doing."

Michael rolled them over and placed himself under Galen. "You do. When you fantasize, don't you think about how you'd like it done?" Michael lightly tickled Galen.

Galen smiled. "Of course. That's Dude One-Oh-One."

"Yes, it is." Michael grinned. "Do to me what you'd want done to you."

Galen felt against his stomach Michael grow a little, talking about it.

"But, no pressure. We do not have to do this. I can wait as long as it takes." He rubbed Galen's back in long, affectionate strokes and kissed him. "If it never happens, we'll cross that bridge. Really. It's okay. I love you."

But the next thing that happened was that Galen's mouth traveled south.

"Let me. Please let me. I want to. I want to give my lover what he wants." Hearing the word "he" come out of his own mouth excited him. It felt right.

He spent the next several moments proving that he had paid attention when he watched other men do it online. And he had taken Michael's words as gospel and performed as though he were giving what he wanted to receive. Michael responded the way Galen had, as though he never wanted it to end.

Galen couldn't believe how easily he had taken another man into his mouth, how much he enjoyed trying to get it right, how grand Michael felt inside of him, how natural the act seemed.

This is mind-blowing. You feel incredible in my mouth. I want to take you all the way in and never let you go.

And he did take in all of Michael. It was ecstasy.

At the end, Galen stayed with him, and drank it all in. He then did for Michael what he enjoyed and didn't remove his mouth right away.

Michael groaned at the extended attention.

When it was over, Galen lay on top of Michael and kissed him slowly and deeply. "That was from another world. You tasted so good. I never thought I could feel like that. Just saying out loud that I had my mouth on you makes me want to do it again."

And he did, for longer that time. Michael moved and moaned and cried out the whole way to the end.

When they were done, Michael offered Galen one more lesson.

He leaned over the side of the bed and dug through the pockets of the sweats he had left on the floor and found his wallet. In it, he located a condom with dogeared packaging.

"As you can see," Michael said, "I haven't used this. I haven't been—"

"Shhh," Galen said. "It's none of my business."

"It is. I want you to know." Their faces were close again. "I haven't been with anybody since I met you," Michael said.

Galen kissed him and was thrilled to finally put Paul and other jealousies out of his mind. "Thank you. Thank you for telling me." They exchanged another long, passionate kiss.

Michael unwrapped the condom and put it on Galen. He created extra lubricant with saliva in his hand. "Love me, Galen," Michael said.

Galen searched Michael's face to see if he meant what he said. He saw longing in Michael's eyes and teasing on his lips and desire in the way he leaned up and kissed Galen.

"You already know what to do. I love bottoming." He whispered, "Fuck me."

I want to fuck you, so bad.

"If you're worried it'll hurt, it won't." He pulled Galen close and whispered into his mouth, "Take me. Come, Baby. Put it in and take me."

And Galen did.

And it was exquisite.

And the pictures finally melded for Galen, Michael's face and Michael's body beneath him, there with him, loving him as he loved Michael.

The union of minds and spirits and bodies, his and *Michael's* body, blew Galen's mind.

He *did* know what to do. He rocked and rocked, feeling Michael's thighs against his own, again and again, and kissing Michael's small, hard breasts, and his soft mouth, and he reached the highest heights of his life, staring at Michael all the time.

At the peak, he spoke Michael's name, as he had dreamt of doing so many times before. He called out, "Michael," again and again. Finally, he shouted the name and let out all the juices inside of him.

And then he whispered the name, over and over, and said, "I love you."

And Galen knew he would never again worry about how he would make love to the love of his life.

A kingdom had opened. The most righteous lovemaking he could imagine was available inside the gates.

There, he would frolic and romp with Michael and explore with him what the kingdom offered.

And he would never again leave it. He had arrived home, to stay for life.

He was homoromantic and homosexual. He was gay.

He felt vindicated against the life he had led and liberated and dizzy with happiness.

He kissed and caressed Michael and murmured his name, and he wondered where life had gone.

Until that point, life had tricked him and tripped him up and goaded him and teased and tormented and even tortured him, years before, when it had taken his parents so cruelly. He had a hard time believing life had really left him alone to exist without interference from it, that life had backed away from him and Michael and let them love one another and drown in each other and exalt their union with trust that would let them build up their love to something glorious and untouchable.

He quickly put the thought out of his mind. He refused to give bad thoughts any room in the front of his mind and turn the best moment of his life into a waiting game, in which he braced for catastrophe.

He and Michael feel asleep in each other's arms and stayed that way until the next morning, when life knocked again on Galen's door and resumed meddling.

∞ Chapter 10 ∞

KNOCK, UNANNOUNCED

IT COULDN'T BE, GALEN THOUGHT, but it was. The person on the other side of the peephole in his apartment door was Georgie.

He had heard the knock and thought it might be a UPS delivery man with a package he expected, even though it was Sunday. Seeing that it was Georgie turned him a little histrionic.

What does she want? Last night I made the best love in the history of the universe, and today, Michael, the most beautiful person alive, and I are going to spend the day glowing about it. We showered, we fed each other scrambled eggs and blueberries, and we're ready to go outside and be alive together and in love together. Please, Georgie, don't take this from me. I'm sorry for everything, but please let me have this. I've waited for it forever, for a lifetime.

Michael appeared behind him and pretended to look through the peephole with him. "How bad can it be?" he joked, not knowing who was there, but Galen didn't smile. He mouthed, "Georgie."

Michael mouthed, "Ohhhh," with a look of mild panic on his face.

Galen had noticed that Michael had a healthy respect for Georgie. Whenever Galen brought up her name regarding some business that still existed between them, Michael became deferential. He looked a little scared.

Galen shrugged, as if to say, "There's nothing we can do," and opened the door. He and Michael were both in view.

The full-figure Georgie—and not the peephole version—was as radiant and carelessly pretty, as always. He hadn't seen her since he had moved out on the evening of the day he had fought with Michael in the police station and Josefina had outed him as being gay. In an odd way, it felt good to Galen to finally see her again.

She looked only at Galen, and the moment turned awkward. He stood there with the person, his new partner, who had, in her mind, replaced her. For Galen, it wasn't that simple. He hadn't merely exchanged one lover for another. He had gone from a livable existence to living life.

"Hi," Galen said. His voice was a little elevated in false cheer.

"Am I going to have to stand out here?"

"No, sorry." He and Michael bumped into each other moving out of the way.

Inside, they stood in a triangle, in silence. It wasn't quite a standoff from a Leone movie, but each was a little awkward. Galen knew Georgie well enough to know she wasn't nervous or daunted by the situation. She had righteousness on her side and nothing to fear. No matter what came up, it wouldn't lead back to her faults, her mistakes. Recriminations would be aimed at Galen.

He noticed something else, though. A lack of arrogance or attitude. She may have been right about everything, but her essence was kindness and not smugness. It made him feel worse. He wondered why she was there. He worked up the nerve to ask.

"Is everything okay?" he said.

She pondered the question for a long moment that stretched the awkwardness.

"I don't know." She sounded a little tired. "I'm not sure."

She was less radiant than moments before.

Galen couldn't lie to himself. He was concerned. She seemed like the wife she had always been, bringing a problem to him. But she also gave off an aura of wanting and needing to keep her distance from him. Her unease wouldn't let her say any more. It made Galen scared more was wrong. He wanted to know why she had come to see him.

"Maybe I should leave," Michael said.

"Don't make me laugh," Georgie said. She never looked at him, but Galen saw something in her face.

"Pardon me?" Michael said. "We—"

"Georgie, what's wrong?" Galen said.

She stared at him as though she were wondering if he really understood what it meant to ask that question. She shook her head at nothing. She seemed to be trying to find a way to believe what went through her own mind.

Galen treaded gently. "Georgie?" He waited for her to look away from nowhere and look at him again. "What's wrong?"

"I'm— We're going to have a baby."

A baby.

A baby.

Galen was astonished. It took him at least half a minute to figure out how to talk.

"A baby…. Are you sure?"

"I'm blue-stick positive."

Those final eight or ten days we were together, before it had broken loose in the police station, had produced a baby. A baby! We were together that morning. I must have miscalculated the dates. Maybe it happened that day!

"I really should go," Michael said. He was visibly shaken, but Galen didn't want him to leave, not then, not with a baby on the way and Georgie standing in his living room, and not after what had happened the night before.

"No," Georgie said. "I'd like you to stay." She finally looked at him. "Even if I do find it ironic you suddenly respect boundaries."

"Okay, I get that it's awkward," Michael said, "but we can be civil, especially with—"

"Civility? You're preaching civility to me?"

Galen looked at Georgie, and something about her face struck him. It was full of pain and worry and trauma. Her façade cracked.

She held her composure, but it struck him for real for the first time, seeing her in person and looking eclipsed by his standing there with Michael, that he had shattered her life.

He couldn't explain it, but he wanted to stand behind her and let her fall back against him. He felt the need to cradle her, for some reason. Maybe it was because she was carrying his baby and he still loved her in his own way.

He reached out, for what, he wasn't sure, but she took a step back and glared at Michael.

"Galen and I have been friends a long time," she said to him. "Even through all of this, we've talked. I know about that first time you kissed, and I have to ask, did it occur to you that you were kissing someone else's husband?"

Uh-oh.

"I don't think I thought—"

"You want respect, but you don't give it. Before I married Galen and wore his ring, if a married man approached me, I wouldn't give him eight seconds of my time, not just for my sake, but for her sake, whoever she was, that poor wife at home, trying to fight through it, with ghosts and shadows of other women who couldn't say no looming somewhere in her marriage. Guys like that were jokes."

Oh, no.

"I would say, 'Go home to your wife.' I wouldn't have spent weeks trying to be alone with him, relying on him for emotional gratification, openly needing him and wanting him to need me back."

"I—"

"Yes, *you*. You, you, you, you, you. Let me guess. You tried to stay away, but Galen chased you. That's the oldest excuse. If you want to stay away, you stay away. And, *I* know love *is* love and that love between two men is just as real and valid and not a game and as much of a threat, or else I wouldn't be standing here telling my husband I'm going to have his baby with his male lover watching. I would think you would have known it, too, and kept your distance."

Michael turned red and looked unnerved and guilty and terribly sad.

Galen held still and waited to see how much more there was, how bad it would be. He couldn't say it out loud to Michael, but he knew it was best to let her talk. He hated having to use his intimate knowledge of Georgie to ease the pain of the man he loved. It was strange.

"When Galen kissed you," she said, "did you push him away? Did you tell him to go home to his wife? Did you care that you were breaking up a family? Did you even have a notion that I was there? That I was at work at a hospital, helping to build our existence as a couple? That I had shifted my life based on faith that my husband would always be there because of promises he made in a church, before God? That you were helping to snatch that out from under me? Even that anyone I knew could have walked down that street and seen my husband cheating on me?"

Neither man answered.

"I'm really glad you're here this morning because I've been wanting to explain something very basic to you."

Georgie, please don't say anything none of us will get over. Please.

"Marriages are weird journeys. Sometimes, you're driving a jalopy, sometimes a Ferrari. The road can be smooth as glass or full of potholes. When the car breaks down, the only two people who should be trying to get it to work again are the people in the marriage. No calling for help unless there's room for both people in the tow truck because they want to leave together. I'm for marriage counseling, but one of them doesn't catch a ride with someone else and leave the other one stranded by the side of the road."

By then, she cried, quiet tears again, like the ones she had shed when she had asked Galen if she had ever made him happy.

Galen's gut wrenched. The guilt ran deep within him. His conscience forsook him, marooned him, left him unable to comfort Georgie because he had no moral compass to guide him in that endeavor.

The tears rolled down her face almost unobtrusively. She talked past them and through them. "There was something about me that worked for Galen," she said. "For eight years, if you count the time we dated. It doesn't mean he's not gay, but anyone married who vows monogamy forever gives up happiness elsewhere. None of us can have everybody or everything. There's always some malcontent in our contentedness. Maybe we search for something, or a vague someone who has something we need, but we don't know who or what that is, so we never find it or him or her or them, and we just keep going. Galen only became unhappy when you refused to do what most self-respecting people would do when someone they're attracted to is married, *committed,*" she paused, "to someone else. Walk away. He might have wanted you, like we all want things, but he would have seen he couldn't have you because you wouldn't have been there, and he would have done what we all do and stayed home and found a way to be happy. Maybe. Maybe. We'll never know."

"Please—" Michael started.

Galen knew Michael was a natural nurturer, at his best with strangers. He probably wanted to hug Georgie and comfort her, even though he was the source of her pain.

"Most people would have let our family come to a self-driven end before they started demanding what they needed from someone else's husband. You texted and e-mailed and called my husband for weeks. You fed him dinner. You practically co-hosted a party with him. *You stood in the middle of the street and kissed my husband not caring about me.*"

"I did. You're right." That honest admission without any defense was the most he could offer since she would never let him touch her, even just to rub her arm and say he was sorry.

She sniffed and gathered herself. "You claim to be an advocate for the marginalized, but you steamrolled right past someone who worried every day about the man she pledged her life to, who supported him in his choice to put his life on the line in his job, even as she saw people get injured and die every week in *her* job…"

Oh, Georgie.

"…who loved the man who told her, yes, they should be parents together and try to have a baby. We made love, often in those few weeks, to try to make it happen, wondering, afterward, whether it had happened."

Her words crushed Galen. She had loved him romantically, as he loved Michael, and the weight of what he had cost her buried him. Her face was soaked in tears. Galen wanted to reach out and wipe them, but he knew he shouldn't. He knew he had no right, and he knew he had to let her experience her side of things her way. Her tears made him feel sorrow and discomfort, but none of that was her problem. He couldn't try to wipe away his guilt by wiping her tears.

He remembered those times he had sex with her and those conversations she mentioned. He had understood later that he had sought intimacy with her because it had become the way he released his pent-up desires for Michael. Doubt about having a child had set in, and he had begun to pull back, but there were those days…those nights…when he needed Michael, and he had sex with Georgie.

And, he had truly looked forward to fatherhood. He had balked at first, but he also had no parents, and the idea of a child, *his* child, his family, fed something in him. She had made him want children, she who was blind to who he was and unable to know what that wish would mean to him, unable to see that he had bargained in secret.

For *he* knew what challenges they faced. He had entered the maze of destiny and known that the more twists and turns he took, the more likely it was he would come out of the labyrinth somewhere where she wasn't, and he had panicked. Something about his kaleidoscopic life had led him to sense he would never be a father, whether it was an earlier subconscious avoidance of taking that step with Georgie because he didn't love her the right way, or whether, by that time, he had had a prescient notion he would end up with a man and possibly never have children. He only knew that he agreed to have a baby with Georgie because he felt it would be his only chance to be a father. He hadn't meant to use her, but he had. He felt deep remorse.

He had figured things out so late, and it had caused a lot of damage, not just to his wife, but to his child, who would be born to parents who would never be together for even one day of his or her life.

He had been unfair to Michael, too, who had to hear about Galen's time in bed with Georgie and her referring to it as "making love". His lover had pursued him as a free man even as he created a baby and formed a permanent tie with someone else. So much time had passed, Galen never would have thought Georgie was pregnant. He couldn't claim to have planned it with forethought about outcomes, but he did feel that by the time he and Michael had made love, the subject of a baby between him and Georgie had long died.

He wanted so much to be alone with Michael to explain it all, to explain the layers. And he wanted to go back to a time with Georgie, during the beginning of his attraction to Michael and his initial inklings that he had traveled on the wrong track in his life, to see disaster looming and behave better to diminish it. He would always feel that Michael and his runaway love for him would make misfortune for Georgie impossible to avoid. But the damage could have been controlled if Galen had read the signs better.

"That's what the marriage you've fought for the right to have looks like," Georgie said. "It's people who share and make decisions and partner up and settle down. It's not just the cliché 'take care of each other when you're sick' thing. It's finally clearing out the garage together. It's listening to a story and getting to the fiftieth 'so then' and still wanting to hear more. It's playing nudge wars with your feet on the coffee table, watching TV, and turning that into sex on the couch."

As much as Galen understood Georgie, he didn't want Michael to be wounded by her tirade. He loved Michael for letting Georgie air her hurts with no defense of himself or his actions, but he sensed doom.

"We might have made it, forever, even," she said. "I mean, do you really think people who are married fifty years don't go through some horrid stretches? But they make. That could have been us, but you inserted yourself, and whatever thin thread of a chance we had to jumpstart our broken-down car and keep driving was gone. Galen's to blame for leaving with you, in your tow truck, so to speak, and leaving me stranded, with a child, but you never should have pulled over in the first place to see what was going on. *We were none of your business.* Galen was *my* business, and I was his."

And I forgot that. I'm so sorry, Georgie.

"I might have let him go, in the end, so he could be happy, but that was for *us* to figure out, based on our vows and promises and history and hopes and wanting to get closure in a way that didn't force us to say and do things we didn't want to so we could have a kind of peace of mind in the future. We entered a marriage. Don't you think we should have been the ones to decide how we exited? We would have known what to factor in or out. You stand there, right now, not knowing for sure what the ramifications are of your intrusion. You've forced a perfect stranger to be stuck with something you dished out, whether I can take it or not and whether it'll haunt me for twenty years or not because you've tailored it to fit *you*, not me, and yet it's my life. That's ridiculous. So, spare me the civility crap."

She had managed to stop crying toward the end of her speech, and she wiped away the last tears on her face.

To Galen she said, "This isn't blackmail because I don't want you back in my life, but you should know I haven't decided what to do about the baby, about whether to have it." She took in a heavy, shaky breath.

He had dreaded a different kind of doom, one involving Michael leaving after what he heard, but she had delivered her own blow.

She doesn't want the baby.

He barely spoke, and it was one word. "What?"

Michael said, "Listen, I know you're angry with me, and rightfully so, but please don't punish Galen because of me."

Galen loved Michael immeasurably in that moment.

"It has nothing to do with you." She said to Michael. "That's been my point the whole time." She turned to Galen. "And I would never use a child as a weapon." Her voice shook, and she blinked away fresh tears.

Galen said, "I know that, Georgie. I know, and—"

"Hang on," Michael said. "I would never accuse you of using a baby as a weapon. I only meant that I would hate to see you make a decision that I was partly to blame for that would, by its nature, work as punishment for Galen. And that's all I meant." She had just read him out, but his tone was full of compassion.

"Either way," she said to Galen, "I would never make this decision to get back at you. This may shock you, but I've done a lot of my own thinking these past weeks, and I'm looking forward and not behind. You were in the wrong life, but I was too. The longer I wallow, the better I feel and the more I can see places where I missed out because you and I were mismatched. I'm eager to move on." She looked Galen dead in his eyes. "I'm not sure I want to take *anything* from my past with me into my future."

Galen knew he deserved her disregard, and he couldn't blame her. She could be free of him forever if she just didn't have his baby.

But he and Michael had just dared to dream about a family. With this news, he was closer than ever to receiving that wish. He didn't know what it would look like with Georgie in the picture, but he wanted the child, his child. Even without Michael, if somehow the previous fifteen minutes had cost him his relationship with the man he loved, he wanted his parents' grandchild.

He wanted his child. He was desperate. "Georgie, *please.*"

"Don't push me, either of you. I'm on my last strength, here."

Galen would bargain hard to keep his baby. "I know it's your right to choose, but I want this baby, Georgie. We can find a way. I'll give you whatever you want, whatever custody and financial arrangements you dictate, but...*a child.*"

She sighed, heavily and wobbly. It was a sigh that held unshed tears behind it. "Well, Gay, a few months ago, a child would have been something else, something unreal." She laughed a little, and a few tears slipped out. "Now...." A deep frown replaced the mirthless laugh. "I don't know. I'm tired. Physically. Mentally." She shook her head in wonder. "I've been reading those baby books." She gave him a sad smile. "I'm a nurse. I thought I knew everything. But I don't. They say growing a baby is the same as going rock climbing every day. Every day." She looked at Galen and reminded him of what she had been like when they met each other. She seemed younger standing there pregnant and worried, and more vulnerable than the formidable Georgie she had become as his wife. "Seems like a miracle," she said.

With that, the import of what he had done hit him hard. She had read baby books. She had wanted to go through a pregnancy with her husband and track the baby's progress with him and show off ultrasounds, at the hospital and the police station, and wonder about the gender, and he had robbed her of that and left her with the most colossal part of the dream that had turned into a nightmare—a child, and the humiliation, of not knowing about her own husband, of having the baby of a man who had clearly never loved her the right way, even as everything she did, demonstrated by a growing belly, showed that she was in it for life. The shame ran deep in him.

"Georgie. I'm sorry, Baby Girl. I'm so sorry."

"I guess I came here," she looked at Michael and choked on tears then looked again at Galen, "to ask my husband what I should do."

At that, Galen's eyes filled with water.

Michael swallowed hard and blinked several times. "I'm also so, so sorry. Everything you said. I...."

"Gay, I gotta go. This was a mistake. Mom and Dad said it would be a mistake. They were right. They're over you, by the way. Whatever initial sympathy they had for the general sadness of it all is gone. They just want me to move on."

"I know. I don't blame them. I just...I don't think they should be making this decision for you, or even for me, even if they can't stand me." He was petrified of his own words. He hoped he hadn't alienated her.

"I know, but you know my family. What do you expect? They're gonna butt in. Especially Tracy. She can't stand you. She doesn't want me stuck with you in my life."

"I know," he said resolutely. "I know." He swiped at the few tears that had fallen onto his face.

Michael couldn't help himself. He reached out and rubbed Galen's shoulder. It was no more sexual or intimate than if a good friend made the same gesture to reassure his buddy, and Galen accepted the affection with relief. But, perhaps in deference to Georgie, Michael dropped his hand.

Georgie watched it fall and stared at them both. "They're right. I can't expect you to be my husband and work this out with me. I have to work it out for myself."

"Georgie, please, we can find a way."

He wept with a quiet calm. She no longer cried. It was as though she lent him her light tears.

"Well, I don't mean to be harsh, but keep a grip on reality and your ego and know that I don't see 'the way' as you and me reconciling. I get where we are, and, anyway, I don't want to be with you anymore, Gay. I know that now. I'm not holding the baby out as hope for us to get back together. Even if you left Michael right this second, I wouldn't accept you back."

"But if I had never left. Is that what you came here to say?"

"Maybe. We'll never know if you would have felt even more trapped. I mean, a trip to Vons for some parmesan cheese was too much to ask. You ditched me then. Would you have ditched me now, with just you and me and baby making three?"

Or would I have seen your glow and loved our child to death and you a little more than I did before, enough to make it through with you? That's what you really came here to ask.

"Like I said, I don't know," she said. "And the fact that I don't know tells me I didn't lose what I thought I did the day Josefina called me with the news."

That was the final blow. Those were the words that told him their life together had been an exercise in futility and brought about unnecessary pain.

She looked at Michael. "Even you're not to blame for whatever kept him from coming home to me and for needing to be with you. You can't ignore nature. I just wish you had had the decency to practice what you preach and respect the love between two people and leave that love alone. You smugly disregarded the love I felt for my husband like it wasn't valid or worthy, like it was a game you could break up, like it was some minor detail in your way, in *your* way while roaming around *my* life, like real people weren't behind that love and in it and around it and leaning on it, with one of them building on it and counting on it and hoping to create a child to benefit from it. Gee. What does that sound like? I'd bet you've heard that before, people trampling over other people's right to love."

She turned to leave. Galen caught her arm. They looked at each other as though no one else existed. It wasn't romantic love they exchanged in the look or even friendship or camaraderie. It was deep familiarity, the kind that comes with a long relationship, with marriage. Messages between them could be shortcut into a single look. They understood each other in those abbreviated moments to the exclusion of others. Inside that hollow realm only they shared, Galen tried to reach Georgie a final time.

"Please consider keeping the baby, Georgiana. Please. And...."

"What?"

"Thank you."

"For what?"

He cleared his throat. It was thick with emotion.

Michael's hand moved, as though he wanted to touch Galen again, but he let it drop by his side.

"For being you. For being the best wife I could have asked for. For being my friend." He gathered himself. "When I met Michael, everything from that point was out of my control. Who I was came out before I did. I didn't so much walk away from you as I walked toward myself." He knew his next words would hurt, but he had to speak them. "I fell in love and found myself. I had lost myself."

"With me?"

"No, Baby Girl, not with you. Probably when I was still in high school. Like I said before, I ran away from who I was and didn't look back. Losing my parents made it easy to hide. I was blindsided by grief and blamed everything I felt on that. And, you know, by the end of college, when I wondered, about one person, there were no excuses, but still I found them. The trial. Later, seeing the photos of my mother. But it was only a matter of time before something, or someone," and he looked at Michael, "made me look back so I could move forward."

"I know. I know." She leaned in and tip-toed and kissed his cheek and wiped the tears from his face. "I know. And I won't play games about the baby. I have to decide very soon."

"How much time?" He thought about the last time they were together. He got flashes of her body and regretted the lies he told, afterward, about the road ahead and starting a family with her.

"A week." She cast her eyes down. He could really tell, then, how tired and worn down she was. He had thoroughly exhausted her. He only saw his own guilt in her face and in her sadness and in her bravery and in her class.

"I won't keep you guessing," she said. "I'll call you, and it will either be after it's done or to tell you I'm gonna have the baby."

He stroked the side of her arm. "All right, but one thing. I don't want you to go through it alone. If you need me there...."

"I know, but I don't want you there. You're the reason I'd be there to begin with. Seems strange."

"Okay." He wiped his face. "Okay."

"Tracy's got me."

"Okay."

They exchanged a sad smile.

"Georgiana?"

"Yes?"

"If you decide not to have the baby, you won't hear a word out of me. I know this really is your decision, even more so, now." He collected himself. "I know it won't be easy, either way. And, you have every right to doubt this, but out of everybody concerned, on this I worry most about you. I don't want you to suffer any more than you have. You don't deserve this, any of it. You'll get no recriminations from me. In the end, *in the end*, I support whatever you want to do."

She cried more tears. "Thanks, Gay."

He nodded and gently wiped her tears. She had finally let him touch her in a meaningful way. "Let me walk you to your car."

"No."

And she left.

After the door clicked shut, Michael headed for it.

"Where are you going?" Galen said.

Michael stood in front of the door. "I'm leaving. I have no choice. I have to get out of here."

∞ Chapter 11 ∞

EBBING TIDES

GALEN PANICKED. HE NEEDED MICHAEL there, with him, for himself and for Michael. He had miscalculated horribly with Georgie, and he didn't want to do the same with Michael.

He said, "A lot just happened. I need you to tell me *precisely* what part of it is sending you away from me."

Michael walked back to him. "All of it. I wrecked your life. You had a life." He raised his voice. "What did we do? To your life? *To your wife's life? To your baby's life?*"

"Nothing that wasn't going to happen anyway."

"Are you sure? I mean, it sounded to me like you two were living a fairy tale, with in-laws, and, what, barbecues and volleyball on Sundays, where you played on opposite sides and teased each other through the whole game? You called her 'Baby Girl' right in front of me!"

"Out of habit!" As soon as he raised his voice, he regretted it. "It's a name," he said more quietly, "not a feeling. Georgie and I are *old* friends."

"Habit? Or love? Whom do you love, Galen?"

"How can you ask that?"

Michael followed his own track of conversation and didn't answer. "She knew so much about what I had done—calling, texting, my dinner party, because you told her. You two can clearly talk about anything, even in conflict. You have a bond."

"Of *friendship*."

"What happened with us last night? Was that love? Or more impulse? The same impulse that married Georgie and agreed to have a baby with her?" His voice shook. He appeared scared to hear the answer.

"Yes, it was love!" He didn't care, that time, that he raised his voice. "Yes, yes, *yes*. I love *you*. I've waited my whole life for you. Even Georgie knows that. She knows me, and she knows that fact now that it's out there. I can see it, and she can see it. The truth is clear. I care deeply for her and love her as a person, and I'm very, very sorry for how things have ended up for her, but I'm not *in* love with her. You *know* this. Tell me you know this."

"Not even with her carrying your baby? She's gonna have your baby. She can…" He sighed and shook his head.

"Say it. Now is not the time to withhold if we're gonna make it."

"She can give you the one thing I can't. A biological child."

"Just yesterday you said you couldn't wait to have children with me."

"And it's still true. Even this child. I really hope she has the baby. But will you be happier that you're sharing it with her, your old friend, and not with me, through some stranger we ask to carry a child?"

Galen put his arms around Michael. "*No.* How can you even ask that?"

"Because you were trying to have a baby with her while you were letting me get close to you."

"It isn't like you think. I didn't know who I was. I fooled myself in both worlds. And you wouldn't even speak to me."

Michael looked away.

"Please look at me." Galen said.

Michael looked at him. He appeared confused and hurt and even guilty, about Georgie and his trepidations toward Galen and the misunderstanding they had caused.

"Despite my past and what I hoped for and even planned for, I never thought I would actually, I mean *actually* end up with a man, in a different life. And you know I don't play the parents card," he said and paused to get hold of his emotions, "but sometimes they aren't a card. I get to be affected by their murders. I get to miss them and talk about how losing them makes me feel. My therapists taught me to never apologize about that."

"I know, and I don't want you to." Michael touched his cheek. "I know."

"Their deaths left me with no real family." He cleared his throat and spoke slowly. "I wanted. A family. I wanted my parents' grandchild. Can you understand that?"

"I can. I can." He kissed Galen's cheek and the bridge of his nose and his mouth and rested his forehead on Galen's. "I understand. I do."

He closed his eyes, and everything about his countenance was full of love for Galen. He was in a quandary, Galen knew. He felt obligated to make it right in multiple directions, and he was torn by competing demands—Galen's need for understanding and Georgie's retroactive right to have Michael cease fire on her marriage, something he couldn't give her, which made it worse.

The worst.

All Galen could do was explain why he had made certain choices and hope Michael understood him and still loved him at the end.

"I wanted to be a father, you know? I wanted to have somebody who belonged to me and to whom I belonged, no matter what, the way my mom and dad and I belonged to each other. So, I agreed to have a child. I lived one life but wanted another—with someone who wouldn't talk to me. In some ways, I thought I was doing what the universe seemed to have planned for me since it didn't look as though you and I would be together."

Michael nodded with a head that hung low.

"I roamed a little aimlessly. It made me reckless and careless. I made wrong turns. I don't know what to say."

Michael didn't respond. He stared at the ground and mulled over what Galen had said. Occasionally, he shook his head a little and laughed a mirthless, incredulous, disgusted-with-himself laugh.

He said, "Did you ever tell Georgie about why you wanted a child? Did that ever come up? I can't imagine she wouldn't listen to everything you had to say, hard as that is for me to admit."

"Don't let it be. Please."

Michael stayed on his own conversation path again. "Why didn't you tell her that just now? It might convince her to keep the baby."

Galen stroked Michael's arm. "I don't think you even get how amazing you are."

"I don't know."

"It's true. And to answer your question, I couldn't tell her. I've hurt her enough, and she's not an incubator. No matter how much I want my child, I can't expect a person to devote their existence to making sure I get what I want, especially not Georgie. I'll either have the opportunity to be the father of a child who will have ties to my parents because Georgie wants to be a mother to *this* child, or I won't."

Michael shook his head. "I'm sorry."

"We'll just have to see what happens."

"At least you're thinking of her in some way. Believe me, I'm not amazing. I knew she was there and ran her over. The first Sunday we hung out, I flat-out harassed you for feeling devoted enough to go home to your wife. *Your wife.* Georgiana. A person with cute names and nicknames that her husband, her old friend, gave her. Of course, she wanted you home. That's why she married you. She had every right to expect you to walk through her front door at the appointed time. I was new to your world and felt put out by the threat of someone else having a hold on your heart, and that person was married to you for years, yet I didn't allow her the same feelings, when she was the only one who had a right to them."

"You have to stop. Stop. This is not your fault."

"I acted like she was unreasonable, when, really, I can imagine how she felt. I could then, and I do now. I showed up at your job after the explosion and full-on derided you for asking me to leave Georgie's space. I was there but somehow expected her not to be. Because, like she said, I didn't take her seriously. You said she was on her way, and I punished you for it. Hypocritical bullshit on my part. She's right. We screwed up. I screwed up."

Galen was scared Michael wanted to do something drastic to make amends. "No, you didn't. I did. You didn't."

"I *did*. No matter how I felt about you and me, when it comes to her, I ridiculed her presence in your life, and she did nothing wrong. That night we kissed in front of my office, I made fun of your having a date with her. I did the same thing that made me angry with you when you asked about Paul, except that was once. I minimized her at every turn. And I ended up with her husband." He laughed at himself. "The two-faced irony! I made her out to seem needy and weak for having the very thing I wanted, the very thing I took, something that was already hers. There's no forgiving it."

"I'm not a toy you took. I'm a person who came to you willingly." Michael's assessment of the situation hurt Galen.

Michael sighed. "I'm sorry. I know, and I'm grateful and lucky. No matter how we got here, I love you." He was despondent. "But this is awful. What I did was awful. I can cut you some slack because of your confusion and the mixed messages from me and from yourself. But for me, there's no excuse."

Michael was off the rails. Galen had to set him straight in his crisis of conscience.

"I know everything she said was hard to listen to," Galen said, "but she got one thing wrong."

"What could that possibly be? What could she have possibly gotten wrong?"

"A marriage was in progress, but not a real one. She and I are extremely compatible when it comes to day-to-day life. Whether it was laundry or dishes or money or politics or what to watch on TV, we got along great."

"I noticed that just now. It was hard to watch. I think that's part of what got to me."

"Well, but maybe we got along too well for our own good. Sometimes people don't argue, like we are right now, because they don't care, not enough, anyway."

"Maybe."

"Sometimes having struggles—and bothering to fight through them—tells you you really love someone. Feistiness and fire come from passion and love. Congeniality can mask a lot. It kept me from seeing that romantic love wasn't there. It hid from us that the bridge between us was faulty in places, the most important ones, the ones that keep the marriage from collapsing. We rarely fought *with* each other because we never had to fight *for* each other. The stakes were never that high. Somehow, we never had something on the line that was priceless and so scary to lose, we'd fight hard for it. If we had had to, we may have seen that we weren't sure it was worth it because we didn't have the right kind of love. It would have exposed what was missing. I mean, we finally came up against something hard, and our marriage ended."

Michael hung onto his words, looking for exoneration, for an out. He shook his head. "Maybe," he said again.

"Not maybe. It's the truth. If we had really been in love, she would have been right, and everything you did would have been wrong. Yes, I'm an annoyingly logical cop, but sometimes it comes in handy, and I need you to hear me."

He grazed Michael's chin with a finger and smiled.

"Last night, you showed me the way. You knew what I didn't, and you showed me the way. I'm the expert on this because it was my marriage, and I need you to let me show *you* that it's okay to let yourself off the hook."

Michael smiled sadly.

"I'm telling you, the premise of her outrage is flawed and false because she and I didn't have that love she accused you of destroying. Maybe, *maybe,* on principle, you could have stayed away, but the door was open because the right kind of love wasn't guarding it and keeping it shut from outsiders, so that it wouldn't have mattered if you had knocked on that door or fled the scene of a marriage in progress. You could have withered in front of that door for a thousand years, starving with a long beard, and we wouldn't have known you were out there if we were safe, *really safe*, inside, protected by…true love, to be a little corny, the way I believe you and I are, because, let me tell you, if any man is out there knocking, I can't hear him. I only see you."

Michael never looked away. He held onto Galen's words.

"If she and I loved each other the right way," he paused to be sure Michael heard him, "the way I love you, I may not have arrested you, which I now know happened because something about you brought me into your universe. That's the only reason I noticed you talking to strangers in the park. The spell was cast the moment I saw you, and it worked because my heart didn't really belong to anyone who could ward it off. And if I did arrest you, just as a cop, I certainly wouldn't have held onto those cell bars or come so near you. I never would have thought to offer you my phone, the thing you say made you fall in love with me. I never would have skipped a date with her, which is what I did—that's what she meant about the parmesan cheese—I left her hanging to give you that ride home— and I never would have invited someone I arrested into my car, such a small, private space. And I *never*," he waited a beat, "*ever* would have told you my story. Ever."

Michael cast his eyes down, but he also nodded a little, accepting the truth of events he had been part of and witnessed.

"Real love is the only thing that can keep a marriage up. You came into my life, and it came crashing down because I'm supposed to be with *you*. Yesterday? At the beach and upstairs and all night? It was perfect. Our life, the life ahead of us, is what is supposed to happen. That's why we're here—"

"And Georgie's not." Michael shook his head. "That wasn't how she saw it, when I first showed up. And that matters."

"It does. But how I see it matters too. What the truth was and is matters most."

"She saw humor and friendship and affection and love and faith," Michael said. "And she gave herself to that faith and because of that faith. She had a marriage. She was living her life."

"I saw those things, too. People can have a relationship filled with humor and affection and even love and faith. It doesn't mean those two people should be married. You said it yourself, that first Sunday. 'If they make the right pledge,' you said. She and I pledged ourselves to the wrong person. We had faith in the wrong life."

"I don't know, Galen. I feel vile."

"And I feel worse than that, but I don't know what we could have done to change it. If you had never shown up, I would still be in a marriage with the wrong kind of love. Eventually, that would have come to light. And even if it didn't, Georgie still wouldn't have the marriage you and I wish she had, or you assume she had. *Every* masquerade ends. Masks get heavy. They fall. The things my marriage hid were exposed. The time had simply arrived. And you arrived along with it."

"That may be true, but are we just fortunate coincidence was on our side? Or worse. Maybe it didn't arrive with me. Maybe I brought it."

"No. Uh-uh. You were not the cause or the catalyst. My real feelings brought all this about. I mean, to put it bluntly, you and I are the effect of the unmasking, and it's a good effect. The other one may be Georgie getting her freedom."

"Didn't we perpetrate evil, not caring how it came out for everyone else, including your child?" It was not a rhetorical question. Michael looked to Galen for the truth.

Galen took a long time to consider the question. "No. I know myself, and I know her. If what she and I had were the real deal, even if I were bi and had feelings for you, it would have stopped in the park. I would have walked right by you without noticing you."

"I don't know."

"I do. You and I weren't 'in it and everything else be damned.' We're here because we started what Georgie and I gave us room to start…and finish. And on a long drive to WeHo, we acknowledged it. We were already in love. There was nothing to do about it."

"Maybe. I can't shake the image of her standing there, crying, about things we did to her."

"I know, and I was childish, chasing after you without thinking long-term, but I still know I didn't go looking for this. It found me, and us. I was confused, not a con artist. I'm gay, Michael. And I'm in love with *you*."

"I'm not sure that's enough."

Galen's heart stopped. "What do you mean?"

Michael walked away.

Galen followed him. "What do you mean? Are you done? How can that be? Especially after last night and everything you said and everything we did and shared? I became whole with you yesterday. You gave me that. Don't take it from me. Don't take what we have from either of us. Don't you want us?"

He waited, but Michael said nothing.

Galen said, "I'm very sorry I brought this down on you, and I'm hoping you can forgive me and see a way forward."

Michael was still silent.

"We may get the gift of a child. Or don't you want my child?"

"Are you kidding me? I would love, absolutely love to raise a baby that came from you."

Galen didn't feel better. Something about Michael wouldn't let him.

"It's not you. And it's *not* that you're having a child with her. I understand that better than I did even just a moment ago. I really want her to keep the baby."

"If Georgie will let me be in the baby's life, if she has it, I think you'd make a fabulous father, Michael. I'd love to raise a child with you. Not just this child, but others, too."

Michael looked terribly sad. "That's the other thing." His voice shook just a little, but Galen heard it. "You called me 'Michael'. You've been doing it all morning. No pet name, the way you called her 'Baby Girl'."

"That's bothering you? Don't you know why I call you Michael?" He smiled with relief. "I think I *am* the worst, boyfriend, that is. I never told you that when I heard your name in the jail cell, when I made you say it again, and you spoke it a certain way while you looked at me, like you were saying it for me, it was part of what drew me in. Michael is a beautiful name, the most beautiful name I've ever heard because it belongs to you. I don't want to call you anything else."

Despite the edgy discourse, they looked at each other lovingly. "I love you, Michael."

"I love you, too," Michael said. "I don't know what to do. A lot has happened. You're asking me to be tied forever to a woman whose life I disrupted on a massive scale. Even if she forgives me, if she has the baby—and I hope she does—she'll always be there in some way. I think I need some distance, some time to think about everything."

"What does that mean?" Galen swallowed hard. "Can't we think about it together? Can't we talk? Let's talk. Forever, if necessary. I want to be with you while we deal with this. That's what real love is about."

Michael headed to the door. "I need to be alone for a while." He opened the door. He looked down and talked to the floor. "I've waited so long…for…" He stared at Galen.

"For what? Please tell me, Michael. You've waited so long for what?"

"For you. And now…." He took in a deep, resolute breath. "She's beautiful, Galen," he said. "Your Georgiana."

Galen watched him leave and felt he would never come back. There was something about the last words he spoke that made Galen understand their fate was sealed.

It somehow seemed right to Galen. He would get what he deserved. He would be miserable forever.

∞ Chapter 12 ∞

GEORGIE ON THEIR MINDS

MICHAEL STAYED GONE FOR FOUR days. And Galen had done what he best knew how to do with Michael. He gave him space and stayed away.

And hurt every day.

And missed what they had started on the beach and in Galen's bed.

And dreaded getting a phone call from Georgie telling him their baby was gone.

So, he worked, and he leaned on Chet with a synched-up schedule and long lunch hours. He took heart in the fact that the one solidly good thing to come from all his problems was a cemented friendship with Chet, who acted as though Galen had always been his gay best friend and who listened to him go on and on about fatherhood and Michael and everything that scared him. They had talked about other things, too, like whether Chet should take the sergeant's exam and propose to Brianna. They weighed Chet's options over multiple burgers and fries and concluded that at least one of them should enjoy marital bliss, and that Chet would be miserable if Brianna weren't in his life for good. Chet would pop the question.

And Galen would patrol and wait, for Michael and Georgie and his child.

And then a miracle happened.

Five days into staring at his phone waiting for good news from Michael and very bad news from Georgie, he came home and found Michael leaning on his front door.

"I get it," he said. "I don't love it, but I think I get it, now."

"Come here," Galen had said, and he had wrapped his arms around Michael, at the front door.

They kissed, and Galen remembered the joy of Michael's soft lips.

They moved their reunion indoors.

Inside, Michael explained his epiphany. "I went to the beach after I left here and walked and thought about everything you said about our being destined to be together."

"The cold air can really clear the mind," Galen said.

"I thought about my behavior. Georgie really hit a raw nerve. I spent almost every moment after I left the beach until I woke up this morning thinking about her words, and yours, and concluding that you were right, and you maybe even missed something."

"I did? I'll take that as good news."

"I don't think your marriage was simply unguarded. I think you unintentionally sent out clues that said you were available. I don't think I would have approached you outside the station otherwise. That's when I fell in love. After that, I was compelled to get in your car and exchange contact information with you and call you and text you and need you."

"That's what I was trying to say. It had happened to us, and not the other way around."

"Yes, it did. And that chain of events matters to me. It's how I can live with myself and with us. We didn't look to cause this."

"No, it was simply done."

"And we followed a path set out for us. It just took me a while to see it. I needed a clear space to think. I had to be sure."

"And are you? I don't want to push you."

"I am. A lot of wrong things happened, but I don't think we were wrong to try to be with each other. I love you. And I need you so much."

"I love you, Michael."

Michael smiled. "My name sounds okay now." He kissed Galen. "We'll get through this," Michael said. "And if Georgie keeps the baby, we'll work through how she'll fit in. As you said, wanting to get through it shows how much we love each other."

"How about we finish our interrupted Sunday?"

And they went upstairs and made love. Galen had no hesitations that time. It was blissful and exciting and desperate. They had found each other, twice, and neither wanted to let go.

As they went on baby watch, Michael surprised Galen and asked him to move into his apartment. At first, Galen worried it might tip Georgie over a precarious edge. Then he realized he was again being selfish. It was better for Georgie to know exactly who her co-parent would be as she thought about whether the keep the baby. Galen would always want to be with Michael. Hiding to appear less together would do Georgie no good and was unfair to Michael. The following day, he packed up what little he had and moved into Michael's apartment. He planned to formally move out after he got past whatever Georgie decided about the baby.

He texted her his new address but made no demands for information. He ended the text with, *I'm sorry to intrude. No pressure. Want to make it easy for you to find me just whenever it works for you. Galen.*

And he and Michael waited.

∞

Six days after Georgie had knocked on Galen's door, she knocked on the door he had shared with Michael for just a day. It was a Saturday. He and Michael were home. She had texted that she would like to come by.

Galen expected very bad news. If she were keeping the baby, she could have called. If she had already ended the pregnancy, she might have felt obligated to explain to Galen in person. They were, in their own way, still friends, and she may have wanted to do him the final courtesy of telling him in person she would not be giving birth to their child.

"Hi, Georgie. Come in."

"Hi." She entered the foyer and looked around. Galen tried to read her face, but her expression was nondescript. She seemed more resolute than happy.

They led her through the hallway and into the living room.

She looked at Michael. "This is a very nice place. I can see you put a lot into making it warm and inviting."

She smiled. The smile was friendly. Galen wondered where she was headed. Six days earlier, she had told off Michael in very raw terms.

"Thank you," Michael said. He returned the smile, a little surprised.

"How are you feeling? Would you like to sit down?" Galen said.

"Yes." She made her way to Galen's favorite chair. When they were seated, she said, "I feel better, and worse. Morning sickness."

"Morning sickness? Does that mean?"

"Yes. The baby's due in July. First week, we think."

She's going to have the baby. I'm going to be a father. The situation isn't perfect, but this child will be.

He wanted to scream out loud, but he tamped down his jubilance. He wasn't yet sure how Georgie felt about her decision. He sensed Michael's energy next to him on the couch. They were ecstatic, but they would wait until they were alone to celebrate.

"Georgie, this is fantastic news," he allowed himself to say.

"Well, you haven't heard everything. You haven't heard what I propose should happen."

Galen's pulse quickened. "What do mean?"

"You said you would agree to anything to have this baby," she said. "Is that still true?"

"Yes, but…." He took in a slow, questioning breath. He realized it sounded like, "I know I said that, but I didn't mean it."

Michael stepped in. "We promised you we would agree to whatever you proposed," he said to Georgie. "We know how hard this is for you. We said no pressure, and we meant it."

"We did," Galen said, but he was already devastated.

"How do you envision us moving forward?" Michael said.

Galen barely heard anybody. He was sure Georgie came to tell them she would rather he not see the child, so she could make a clean break. And he would keep his word and agree to her terms, but a part of him died inside. He feared he'd never be able to revive it.

She took a long time to answer Michael. She glanced around the room, as though she planned to buy the apartment.

"This really is a very nice home."

Galen wished she would deliver the bad news.

"You're kind," Michael said. "I saved a lot of years to be able to buy it. My mom and my aunt and uncle smoothed the way, but it's mostly me."

"It's good to have family helping out." She glanced at Galen, but she still mostly spoke to Michael. "You've been at your job long? Galen always made it sound pretty important."

What is this, a job interview? Can we please get on with the bad news?

"I wouldn't say important in the usual meaning. Maybe critical to the people we help. I guess what we do is important to them."

"My job is the same way. I'm a nurse."

"Galen mentioned it."

"No one cares what sick people need, not really, not in a caretaker way. It can be something as minor as Chapstick, but it can change their whole day, just ending that little bit of discomfort. They will think of nothing else until they can find a nurse to help them with that small thing."

"Wow. That's what I say to people, too." Michael said. He smiled at Georgie in a way that, for a moment, cut out Galen. He kept talking, just to Georgie. "They wonder when we ask for donations and we say we're going to buy Vaseline, but those little things are huge to someone who's sick or exposed or who may feel they're never going to get that one item they need. Everything comes from someone else. The wait can be maddening and even scary, depending upon what they're waiting for."

It dawned on Galen that they were both natural caregivers. He had probably been able to relate to Michael partly because he had spent years married to a nurse. He was pleased they got along, and under different circumstances, would have sat back with joy and watched them gel, but he couldn't focus on any of it. He wanted the bad news sooner rather than later.

"Georgie, please. What are your terms regarding the baby?"

She looked down and rubbed her stomach then looked up.

"I think the best course of action is for me to have the baby and for you to take full custody and let Michael adopt it and be the other legal parent."

They gasped in unison.

Georgie smiled warmly. "Gay, I've thought about this. And, actually, it was Tracy's idea." She looked at them both. "But once she planted the seeds, I felt the load lighten, and I imagined it, and it makes sense."

They were still too stunned to speak.

She looked at Michael. "I said my piece with you and made my peace. I'm past my issues there. I wasn't looking for my old life with my rant. I wasn't looking to change things back to how they were. I didn't want that, and I don't want that. I really had just needed to say those things and get them off my chest. I felt it was my right."

"Of course, it was. I would never argue with you about that," Michael said.

"And, I guess out of self-respect, I couldn't let anyone think they could so boldly cross my boundaries without me saying anything."

"I understand. Way more than it may seem."

"And you had made me listen to you by suddenly being in my life, without my permission, and I thought the least you could do was listen to me without me asking for yours. And you did. In the end, though, I know nothing that happened to us was your fault. It just happened."

Galen couldn't believe what he heard.

"And I don't resent either of you, really. I'll always hate the way events unfolded, but I think the reasons for those events were out of our control."

She held them captive with her generous words.

"I'm eager to move on, though. I don't want to have ties for twenty years or fifty years, as we share a child. But I would never give up a child of mine for blind adoption. So many mothers have no choice but to give up their child. I see it every day, but I have a choice. I love this baby, and I'm capable of raising her, if that's how this plays out. But if I let her biological father raise her—"

"Her?" Galen said.

"Oops. Yes, her. The benefits of working at a hospital. It's a baby girl."

"A girl. A girl!" Galen beamed. "A girl!"

Michael grinned. "That's awesome," he said to Galen. "A little girl." He laughed with delight. "A little baby girl. Wow."

"Pretty amazing," Georgie said. "And, you know, if I let you raise her, *and you promise to keep me in the baby's life,* the way a lot of biological parents know their children who were adopted by others, then I'll be okay."

"I don't know what to say," Galen said.

"Neither do I," Michael said.

They both beamed.

"Actually, I do know what to say," Galen said. "It's very generous, Georgie."

"Well, I don't know how generous it is. But I can't see *not* having a child growing in me, yet I feel it will be healthier for everyone, especially for the baby, if I move on and let her be raised by two happy parents who love each other." She looked at Galen and spoke gently. "I couldn't take your family from you, Gay. I know what this child will mean to you."

Galen was too choked up to speak.

"All I ask is for you not to turn it acrimonious and stupid if I want to see a Thanksgiving play or if I ask for a school picture. She doesn't need to know about me until you two think the time is right. I'm not asking to be a confusing presence who shows up just when she's having a teen moment to take her to Disneyland. I don't need regular contact or access, not if she's with you."

"Are you sure? Are you sure you can live with that?"

"I'm positive. I just need peace of mind that I don't have to be scared about what happened to her or how people are treating her or where she even is, and this kind of adoption will let me have it. Don't vanish with her, is what I'm saying. We can be like divorced parents who live in different states and agree that the children will live with one over the other, except I won't be in the picture even that much. I'll let you raise her your way, without interference. I won't have legal rights. I can work with any limits you set as long as I know she's safe, at an address I can find, with two loving parents."

Galen looked at Michael, who nodded eagerly.

Galen was joyous and tearful. "You got it. Thank you, Georgiana. Thank you."

"Well, you have to thank Chet, too."

"Chet?" Galen said.

"I can't lie, and don't be mad at him, especially since he put his job on the line, but he wanted this whole thing over. He knew you wanted the baby, and he leaked it to me that you," she looked at Michael, "also seemed ready to start a family, with Galen. He says you're a good person, based on what he's observed. To prove it, he ran you through some databases." She shrugged a little, imitating embarrassment she didn't feel, which her face revealed. "It's my child. I had to be sure."

"Are you kidding? I would have expected nothing less. I work with troubled people. People can have so many hidden problems that can be dangerous."

"Exactly." She smiled gratefully.

"If there's anything else you want to know, just ask. Please. Any time. References, phone numbers, tax returns, bank statements, medical records, hell, my gas station receipts. Anything."

They all laughed.

"And," Michael said, "I don't want to take away from what I know is for your child, and I would never presume anything," he said, "but please let me also say thank you. This is an incredible gift, and I promise to work to make you never regret it." His face signaled he had more to say. "And, I'm sorry. For what it's worth, your words really hit home. It was a dead-on bullseye. I've struggled, and I want you to know I'm very sorry for treading on your life. Everything you said was true, and I have a lot of remorse about it."

"I see why Galen likes you." She smiled and got teary. "Sorry. Pregnancy. Makes me so weepy. I'm crying at car commercials."

They laughed.

"Like I said," she said, "it just happened. I'm past blaming you. And I've been away from Galen for a while, now, and am doing better than I thought I would be. I do appreciate the respect your apology shows. That does mean something to me, just as a person. But I'm going to maybe surprise you."

Galen felt Michael tense a little.

"You've got to let it go," Georgie said, "even if just for the baby's sake."

Again, she had shocked them.

"But it's okay to let it go for your own sake. You have my blessing to let it go. Really. Galen and I were gonna hit this wall at some point. Maybe we should all feel lucky that it happened this way. It showed me I can have a better life, and it's allowing me to let a baby who innocently came into all of this before anyone figured out the timing wasn't great be raised away from hostility. Your presence is part of why this will work. Imagine if Gay and I were simply divorcing and tearing the baby in two. Let's all get our glasses to half full." She smiled warmly.

"Galen talks a lot about what good friends you and he are. I can really see why. You are…something else…Georgian…I have such a strong urge to call you Georgiana. May I?"

She smiled. "Yes. Strange. I like that." She said to Galen, "Don't be mad at Chet. He's on your side."

"No, I'm gonna hug him when I see him." He turned to Michael. "What do you say? Are you ready for all of this?"

"Before you answer," Georgie said, "it sounds like you're more than on board, but I want to say that, ultimately, you don't have to agree to adopting the baby for me to let Galen have sole custody. Legally, he'll be her father, no matter what."

"I understand, and I appreciate that. And I am more than ready for this. I can't wait." He wore a huge grin. "Look at this apartment. It's huge. I always meant to build a family here. I hope it's okay to say Chet's right. We *have* talked about raising a family. Letting me be the baby's father, legally, is an incredible gift. I'll never forsake it. I promise. And, barring an earthquake, I don't think we ever plan to move from here."

"No," Galen said.

"My foundation doesn't have branches around the country," Michael said. "I put all my energy into just one home base here in L.A."

"And my pension is tied to the LAPD," Galen said. "Even if we had to leave this building, we wouldn't leave the city."

"Exactly," Michael said.

Georgie smiled and nodded. "Okay." Her eyes were a little wet, but she looked happier than she did sad. "Okay. It looks like you better start thinking up names for a girl." She stood up, signaling she was ready to leave. "Do you mind if I ask one more favor?"

"Anything."

"Can I have a tour? I just want to know where she'll be."

"Absolutely."

They showed her around the apartment and let her stay a long while and absorb the environment and memorize knots in the hardwood and take in the smells and see all of what she could see from the view out of the living room window, a view her child would one day see.

When she was ready to leave, at the door, she said, "I'll put it in writing. The adoption will be formal and legal. Either of you are welcome to come to any of my doctor's appointments. But if it's okay, Tracy's going to be my birth coach. I want her in that room with me when I go through labor. That part belongs to me." She smiled.

"Of course," Galen said. "Whatever you want. And…."

"I know. And you know something else? I really hope she looks like your mother." She touched his arm.

He hugged her. After the hug, they lingered a moment. Finally, Galen said, "Let me walk you to your car."

She laughed a little. "No."

They laughed too.

"Bye," she said.

"Bye," they said.

"And, Georgie?" Galen said.

"Yes?"

He looked at Michael and then at Georgie. "I hope you'll both allow me to say this and that you'll understand how I mean it." He looked only at Georgie. "I love you, Georgie."

"I know. I love you, too."

He bent his knees a little to look into her eyes and said, "You need anything, *anything*."

She nodded and her eyes filled with water. "I know. I know."

He tipped up her chin with a gentle finger. "Anything. Somebody crosses a boundary…."

"I know."

"Anyone. If anyone gets it twisted…."

She nodded and her tears spilled over. "I know."

"As long as I'm alive, for the rest of your life, Georgiana, you'll never be alone, do you hear me? You don't let anyone think otherwise, or they'll hear from me. Day or night, you call, and I will lower the boom. You don't go it alone, do you hear me?"

"I do," she nodded. "I know, Gay. I know."

"I mean it, Georgiana."

She nodded and couldn't say more.

She touched his face and left.

For a few moments after the door shut, Galen stared at it. Then he turned to Michael, who smiled and nodded and said, "I understand. I get it," and they embraced hard.

After a while they kissed. And they celebrated.

They were going to be fathers. Georgie would do one final act as someone who had really loved Galen. She would give him family to help fill the void losing his parents created, and she would go on to another life.

"Let me say it again," Michael said. "She's beautiful."

"Yes, she is." He pulled Michael close. "And so are you. So beautiful."

"I love you."

"I love you."

∞

Later that day, Galen made a phone call. He was nervous as the phone rang, but he wasn't embarrassed. He accepted that he would face those conversations many times and waited with a racing heart for someone to answer.

"Hello?" came the voice on the other end.

"Hi, Aunt Jeanine. It's Galen, with some news."

∞

The baby was born in July.

And Galen saw his mother again.

And his father and maternal grandparents, the ones who took care of Galen after he lost his parents.

He saw Georgie, too, and was glad.

And he saw those people who had meant so much to him in the strangest places in his daughter. He saw them in her elbows and eyebrows and pinky fingers and gorgeous brown eyes. He was reminded that his mother had had an elegant profile and that his father had a sturdy chin and that his own eyes were more inquisitive than he realized.

He swelled with the emotion of who his daughter was and of becoming a father.

I have a daughter. She's mine. And Michael's.

"Promise me something," Michael had said to Galen when they had only known her for three or four minutes.

"Anything."

"If there's ever a hint of danger coming her way, you go cop immediately."

"Without question."

"You give the other guy no safe quarter, no breaks."

"None."

"If anyone hurts her…"

"Not on our watch."

"Okay."

But they disagreed about the name. Galen wanted to name her Michaela Galena, long for Michael and Galen, in that order. It was a subconscious way of cementing for him and Michael that she would always be their daughter.

Michael wanted the same names for the same reasons, but in reverse. Michael spoke Spanish and had known that Galena meant "small intelligent one". He found out that in the English use, it meant "festive party".

"Come, on! That's a perfect name!" he had said.

But Galen had said that since the baby would have his genes, he would have an unfair advantage if his name prevailed. He thought if their daughter grew up named after Michael, her identity would come from both, equally.

Michael gave in. They named their daughter Michaela Galena.

Georgie had kept her promise and let Galen and Michael become the baby's legal parents to the exclusion of all others, including Georgie. They took Michaela home the day after she was born, although, for eight weeks, Georgie agreed to pump mother's milk that Galen retrieved in a small cooler every morning from her doorstep. "Milk man" jokes flowed in all directions.

The farther into her pregnancy she had gotten, the more independent Georgie had become. She had reached a place where she was no longer sad about Galen. It had started the day she told them they could raise Michaela and had grown from there. The occasional contact with Galen during the pregnancy removed the final romanticized feelings she had for her prior life. It made the break less sudden and less something done to Georgie, without her consent.

Michaela, ironically, had given Georgie a kind of freedom from longing for what could be. She had been allowed to exit somewhat on her terms, and that recapturing of some control over her destiny had made it easier to turn away to a new life. She had come a long way from Josefina calling her to tell her her marriage had ended.

Toward the end of the pregnancy, she had begun to move on with someone she met at the hospital. He had been a visiting physician, intending to stay for six months, but after he and Georgie became serious, he applied for a permanent position and was accepted. His name was Richard.

They had met under odd circumstances. Word had circulated among employees that Georgie planned to give up for adoption the baby she carried. Richard had approached her in a break room and awkwardly asked, "Are you the one giving up your baby?"

After he apologized, they had a real conversation. The more he learned, the more he admired her. Time spent together fostered the beginnings of a love match. Georgie moved cautiously, and so did Richard. They took things slowly until after the baby was born and they could see more clearly what was between them.

Galen and Michael liked Richard. He was in his mid-thirties, and he had been there for Georgie, not only when the pregnancy got heavy and uncomfortable, but to remind her how incredible she was.

There had been a moment when Galen worried that Georgie might have wanted to keep the baby and raise her with Richard, but Georgie truly felt that Michaela would have a better life with two fathers and no outside interference, as agreed, than with four parents fighting for ground.

Galen didn't fully exhale until Michael's adoption of Michaela was finalized and she carried both of their last names. Then, life was complete.

As more time passed, he no longer identified with that time in his life when he had been married to Georgie. He never experienced those moments he had before, when he wondered where he was supposed to be. He loved being gay and living gay. Everywhere he went—work and in his community and online—he openly identified as gay.

He wasn't attracted in the hunter's sense to anyone but Michael, but he saw how men were appealing and how he had likely been attracted to them always and told himself it was something else, admiration or envy of looks or affection for a friend.

Four months after Michaela was born, Galen and Michael were married in a ceremony that included just Chet and Brianna and a few fellow cops and Galen's Aunt Jeanine and Uncle Clayton and their kids and their families on Galen's side, with Michaela as an honorary flower girl, but with dozens of friends on Michael's side, including some who had been or were still homeless, and even more

family members. It was Michael's first—and only, he was sure—
wedding. People flew in from everywhere. Galen had, again, married
into a huge family.

His physical life with Michael was healthy and natural and felt
right. He learned a lot. Michael taught him, and it became second
nature to him. To live with a man and cook with a husband and
divide household duties with him and share bathroom space with
him and enjoy that his husband felt chivalrous toward him—so that
he wanted to protect Galen and kill the spider and take out the trash
and put gas in his car, with Galen feeling equally valiant, the cop who
would shield his husband and family against all others—and to
think about how he, Galen, would take care of his lover and mate
and best friend in old age, as a soulmate in love, and as a dutiful
spouse who had made the right pledge, made Galen feel normal for
the first time in his life.

If Michaela had a favorite father, Galen guessed it was
Michael, which made him happy. She was comfortable with them
both and comforted when she cried by either of them, but there was
a thing that happened when Michael took her in his arms and her
little cheek rested in the crook of his neck. She closed her eyes, and
her problems seemed to disappear, to be replaced by sweet dreams.

Michael had grown so attached to Michaela, that Galen was
grateful every day that Georgie had agreed to cede her territory so
that Michael had a firm footing as Michaela's other parent. He loved
that the man he cherished had been given the gift of a child to love.

They had both taken paternity leave in those first three
months, and although they were tired and slept when Michaela slept
and saw very little of the beach, they were contented. When they
returned to work, they had found a loving nanny who came to their
apartment every day, and slowly, they carved out date nights and
synched up their days off and slipped in their wedding, which they
had largely planned during the pregnancy, and loved each other

through the sleeplessness and fears that all new parents conquered, and relished the love between them that had come out of nowhere, out of a park and a jail cell and a car ride to WeHo.

Occasionally, as he walked through WeHo with Michael and Michaela, Galen wondered how many of the people he saw walking alone had missed their encounter with their soulmate because they took a different bus or caught a later movie or stayed a little too long in the grocery store and arrived at their next destination just after their soulmate had left, and he was grateful for the serendipity of his cop's beat running into Michael's life in the park.

After a few years, they brought a son into their midst, created by Michael, with the help of a safe and sane surrogate and doctors, who performed the conception. And, still, there was room for all of them in the WeHo manse. It overflowed only with love.

They again named their child after Michael, using four letters from his name and calling their son Liam. They thought it would make Liam feel like he belonged as much as Michaela if they were both named after the same father. They figured that way, there would be no subconscious taking of sides, with their children lining up behind the father from whom they took their name. Galen had started their family, and Michael had completed it with a beautiful boy who had Michael's spirit and confident brow. Michael would raise, it turned out, two little fighters.

And Galen couldn't wait for the day when his children were old enough to hear the story, when the daughter and the son of a downtown rescuer who took on the pains and problems of others and a cop grew up and asked how it came to be that Michaela's biological father had loved a man, yet she existed, and Liam had followed.

He would tell them he had wandered with a friend in search of his destiny, and then came Michael, and he knew he had looked so long for destiny because it was out searching, too, for him and

Michael and Michaela and Liam. He would tell his children how glad he was that after chasing destiny 'round and 'round, somehow, it had caught up to him and found them all. In WeHo.

THE UGLY POST

A love story that will grab you and not let you go until you know how it ends.

Charlie and **Bryce** have been together seven years. They don't have it all, but they have all they want—each other and the only relationship that's ever meant anything to them. The week they met, they didn't flirt with seduction to see what would happen. They fell in love and proved it the only way they knew how. They've never been apart since that first tumble into life as lovers, playful partners, best friends, and soul mates.

Charlie has no reason to believe arriving home ahead of Bryce on a random Monday night will change everything between them. But when Charlie logs onto a computer he shares with Bryce, he stumbles into the devastating truth about their relationship.

Or does he? Charlie is sure he's discovered a secret Bryce has kept for seven years, but Bryce swears Charlie is wrong. Blindsided by lies, mistrust, and shattered faith, the two are swallowed into a vortex spinning so fast, it tears them apart. Can they reveal the fiction in the truth and find their way back to each other, or will the black-and-white portrait one man's words paint destroy them forever?

For fans of stories where you're the fly on the wall watching two people who love each other madly "go through it".

CARRY THE ONE

SAILOR PENNIMAN

A CITY OF ANGELS ROMANCE

Tobias knows what it means to get kicked around. One bank took his home, the other, his car. After two hard years of barely hanging on, jobless, the former math teacher lives on Spring Street in downtown Los Angeles in a roomy tent fully outfitted with as many comforts as his last paycheck would provide. When Tobias encounters **Arthur** getting robbed and beaten by three thugs in Grand Park, he can't help but come to the rescue, especially since Arthur seems newly homeless and dangerously clueless.

Arthur sees that night through a lens of drunkenness and can't remember much of it. He is surprised the next morning when he awakens in the cozy tent of Tobias, who saved him from a violent mugging and possibly a stint in County Jail for vagrancy. When Arthur, a lonely man who has longed for a real human connection for fifteen years, realizes that Tobias believes he has nowhere to go, Arthur continues the charade to be near Tobias. His clever scheme works, and Tobias allows Arthur to come closer than anyone ever has.

But Arthur harbors more than one secret, and after finding a clever way to remain in Tobias's life, he digs a far deeper hole of deception without meaning to. Worse, he knows that if Tobias learns the truth, Arthur will lose all access to the man with whom he has fallen deeply in love. Can he keep the mystery hidden long enough to make Tobias love him, no matter what? Or will what started as innocent duplicity destroy the only love Arthur—and Tobias—have ever known?

ABOUT THE AUTHOR

Sailor Penniman lives in Los Angeles and writes modern literature short stories, novellas, and novels. Born in the heart of the city, Sailor enjoys featuring Los Angeles in a story's narrative, wherever possible, and using the city's diverse palette of life circumstances to weave tales of love, perseverance, and equality.

Follow Sailor Penniman on Twitter: @sailorpenniman

(http://www.twitter.com/sailorpenniman)